Keith Fisher was born in Birmingham in 1940 during the bombing. In 1952, he passed the 11 plus examination allowing him to go to a grammar school in Smethwick.

After he left school, he worked in chemical laboratories and did his degree part time. After graduation he went to Canada to start a post-graduate degree which he finished at the University of London with a PhD in Chemistry. In Canada he attended the University of Western Ontario and visited many areas of Ontario.

After his PhD degree, he spent five years in the US (mainly the Midwest). He often visited Canada as he lived just south of the border in Wisconsin, Iowa and Illinois respectively.

After years in Africa, he spent two years in Canada as a visiting professor before moving to Australia in 1989. He travelled extensively in Canada visiting Montreal, Quebec City and Vancouver.

His storytelling skill comes from his Uncle Percy who was a great storyteller and who stirred Keith's interest in short stories. Often short stories are as much about the place as the people involved. These stories involve people from Birmingham (Brummies) who settled in Canada.

This is a work of fiction. Names, characters, businesses, places, events and incidents are either the products of the author's imagination or used in a fictitious manner. Any resemblance to actual persons, living or dead, or actual events is purely coincidental.

Brummies in Canada

Keith Fisher

Brummies in Canada

Vanguard Press

To my Canadian friends Elmer and (the late) Mary Jo who I first met in London Ontario. Later Elmer helped me get a job in Canada.

To my first wife Janet, my daughter Teresa, who was born in Canada and has lived there for many years.

To my son and daughter Alex and Sarah, my stepsons Maxim and Nazar who have all visited me in Canada. To my second wife Ela who has lived in Canada with me and now lives with me in Australia

I wish to thank Elmer Alyea for his photograph used on the book cover. I also wish to thank my Canadian friends Phil and Midge Dean for helpful words of encouragement.

Thanks also to my school friends Tony Homer (US) and Dave Lawrence (UK) for reading some of my stories and giving useful comments.

Contents

Coffee Bar

It was Saturday afternoon and Roy was on his way home to change clothes and go to the Reza (dance hall) for the evening dance. He was hoping to see some friends and hopefully meet some girls. He jumped on the B89 Midland Red bus in Smethwick; he lived near Dudley Rd. Hospital. As he climbed the stairs he was not in a good mood until he spied a girl he had not seen for a couple of years, sitting on the back seat. That brightened his mood and put a spring in his step.

"Hello Roy, long time no see."

"Hello, Maureen, may I sit next to you?"

"Yes, I am going to Birmingham; where are you going?"

"Dudley Road Hospital—I live near it not in it. Are you going shopping in Birmingham?"

"No, I am meeting some friends in a coffee bar behind the Cathedral. We meet there and decide what to do in the evening. We all work at the same place which is near the coffee bar. We generally go there after work before we go home. Today being Saturday, we will meet and decide where to go in the evening."

"I am studying chemistry at Gosta Green, and I am in Birmingham every working day. I might try and look you up after work. I think I know how to get to the coffee bar."

"You are welcome, and this looks like your stop."

As Roy left the bus, he was kicking himself that he had not fixed up a date. He now wished he had stayed on the bus to Birmingham, which would have given him more time. A couple of years ago he'd had a crush on Maureen. Now he renewed his interest. She was better looking than he remembered. He would have to check out this coffee bar, he had a rough idea where it was.

One lunchtime, he walked from the college to the Cathedral. Behind the grounds was Temple Row where he found the coffee bar. Back at college he had a class till five p.m. and then he was free. Roy was unsure what he was expecting as he walked to the coffee bar. Looking in the window he could not really see Maureen but decided to go in anyway. As he entered, he saw Maureen with two other girls.

"May I join you ladies, and may I buy you a coffee?"

After a few sniggers Maureen asked permission from her lady friends. Roy was introduced to Stephanie and Ann. They declined the coffees. As he went to the counter to order his coffee, he heard some hushed conversation which he assumed was about him. He was not too keen on the coffee bar, but he was here for a purpose and had to get Maureen alone. Sitting with three attractive ladies was certainly better than going home on the bus.

Maureen was his interest, but Ann looked a good second. Stephanie was rather petite and younger than her companions.

They asked him about his studies and when he mentioned chemistry, they all said it was a subject they never understood. He tried to explain about chemistry but that was not a good move. Roy explained that the company he worked for had given him a year off to study full-time on full pay. They all thought that very generous. Their company allowed one day a week at college to do shorthand and typing. After completing their courses, they had all got a raise and worked full time. Stephanie was still completing her course. Maureen thought that Roy was courting someone, but Roy explained he and his girlfriend of two years had broken up. The ex-girlfriend thought he spent more time with chemistry than with her. He tried to explain that chemistry would be his profession for his working life, but she would have none of it. He was sad but not heartbroken as their interests were very different. After being unattached for a couple of months he had met Maureen and he was glad that he was now free to do as he wished.

As they finished their coffees, they were all ready to go home. This was Roy's chance as he would catch the same bus as Maureen. Walking with Maureen to the bus stop, he realised anew that she was a very pretty girl, probably better looking than his ex-girlfriend. As they waited for the bus Maureen asked if he was doing anything on the following Saturday. The girls were going to the Reza (that dance hall at the reservoir) and the other two had dates. Roy couldn't believe his luck as he had still been pondering how to ask for a date. Obviously, Maureen had asked about his courting, so she was interested. Roy explained that he had a car, but it was being fixed so he couldn't pick Maureen up from her house. She was not displeased as they would all meet in the city and they could meet him at the Reza. He lived fairly close to the Reza and his walk was not too far. His main worries were how he would take Maureen home and if they would dance together.

At the Reza, he met them all and was introduced to Stephanie's boyfriend and a man introduced by Ann as a friend. Stephanie's boyfriend was the controlling type and Stephanie seemed to be intimidated by him. Ann's friend was a curious character who seemed to have an opinion about nothing. Ann did not seem too interested in him and he seemed to be there to pass time. Roy was enjoying dancing with Maureen although it took a time to get in sync. Roy bought some drinks and Maureen said she could only have one gin and tonic; this was going to be a cheap night out. They all sat at a table and discussed lots of subjects none of which interested Roy; his only interest was Maureen. At the end of the night, they all went their separate ways and Roy rode the bus to Quinton with Maureen. It was quite a walk to Maureen's house, but Roy was enjoying her company. The walk ended up with a kiss and a cuddle outside her house. Roy had a long walk home, but it passed swiftly as all he could think about was Maureen.

Roy's cousin fixed his car so he could take Maureen out on several dates. He would pick her up and go wherever she wanted. The dates all ended with a kiss and a cuddle and a minor feel. Roy just liked being with Maureen and did not want to overplay his hand. His old 1937 Ford was doing a good job, but he thought that he should get a better car after his exams. Maureen loved to go to Clent Hills and his old car struggled sometimes. She loved to sit on the hills and look over Birmingham and Roy was enjoying both views. Actually, he was enjoying the peace and quiet. This courtship was so different from his previous one. The first one involved always doing something but this one involved a lot of doing nothing. This courtship was relaxing not stressful. Besides her good looks Maureen always smelt good.

Exam time was coming, and Roy explained he needed time to do some studying. Maureen did not seem to mind. In this was she was also different from his previous girlfriend. Maureen was very understanding. After one exam session he joined the ladies in the coffee bar. He said he was exhausted, and Ann asked whether it was worth all the stress. He said that if he passed these exams he would get a degree, which would mean a better job and a better life. The girls were impressed with his ambition. They knew no one with a degree. After the exams, Roy took Maureen to an Indian restaurant in the city. She loved the food and the music. His first girlfriend had not liked the food and hated the music. Actually, she seemed to dislike anything he liked. She made known her opinions often in strong language seemingly intended to hurt Roy. Maureen was so refreshing.

After the exams he had to go back to work in Langley not far from Maureen's home. Work in the lab was a regular nine to five. When he used the car, it was easy to pick Maureen up in the evening from her home. This courtship was not going far but he just loved her company. They could talk about anything without getting agitated. He talked a little about work, but she always seemed interested.

Things were changing at home and Roy's family were moving to a new house in Stourbridge. Roy had to help and that cut down on his time with Maureen, but she understood. The new location was no problem for Roy, with his car it was easy to get to work and easy to get to Maureen. He could also use the train when his car gave problems and that was quite often. Luckily his cousin was a mechanic.

On one date they went to the Princess cinema in Smethwick, their first date at the pictures. Maureen cuddled up close and he did not care about the film.

Maureen had chosen the film, so he enjoyed it with no memory of what it was about. He had no car that night, but Roy could escort Maureen home and catch the train home at Smethwick Junction. He was using his car less as it was giving problems. Finally, he sent his '37 for scrap and bought a newer car, a 1949 Ford.

His exam results came in positive, and he had a degree. He invited the ladies to a meal in a Chinese restaurant in the city but only Ann showed up. Here he was with two lovely ladies, and he could treat them to the best meal on offer. He had brought his car so he could take Ann home. He was very fond of Ann; she had a beautiful smile, and her sense of humour was to his liking. Of course, Maureen was the main attraction but having a meal and a good time with two ladies was such a pleasure. Even the waiters sensed they were celebrating something.

At his next encounter with Maureen, he had some bad news. His company had only given him a small raise; he had a degree and expected more. Maureen understood but his anger started to affect their relationship; he could talk about nothing else. One of his mates at work told Roy that this had happened to a fellow a few years earlier. This fellow had left and gone to university on a post-graduate degree course. His mate thought that the company had seemed generous but was probably getting some kind of tax rebate. This set Roy in motion: he contacted one of his classmates who had gone to a university in Canada.

This fellow had only praise for the courses he was taking. Roy wrote to the university and received an invitation to become a graduate student and a teaching assistant.

Roy suddenly announced that he was going to Canada. He explained that one of his friends was there doing a post-graduate degree and loving it. When he told Maureen, she wished him the best of luck saying she was not going to try to stop him. Roy had a new preoccupation and they saw less of each other as Roy planned his emigration. Their last meeting was at the coffee bar. Roy apologized to Maureen for his recent behavior, and said he had been angry. Ann was very interested in his travels and Maureen was wishing she was going.

Roy promised to write to Maureen when he was settled. He was regretting leaving Maureen and was thinking he could have done things differently. His departure from Birmingham to Liverpool was tearful as both Maureen and Ann wished him goodbye. Roy was booked on a liner, and this was the biggest ship he had ever seen. He found he was in a four-berth cabin but as the ship was not full, he only had one cabin mate. Roy had a great journey on the liner from Liverpool to Montreal. The only problem was that there was no one his age. The food was good, but the entertainment was more for the middle-aged passengers. He did make friends with some of the crew, but he was now wishing Maureen was with him.

As soon as he landed in Quebec, he sent Maureen a letter. Now he was really missing her; if she had been with him, they could have had a wonderful time on board ship. He was not sure of his new address, but she would get more letters. There was plenty to write about as the trip down the St. Lawrence to Montreal was magical. Disembarking meant he was going to Toronto by train and then to London. His first impression was that everything was so clean, and people were so polite.

Maureen received several letters and was anxious to reply but she had nothing worth writing. Her mother was asking about these letters from Canada, but all Maureen would say was that they were from a friend. Ann was very interested in the letters and Maureen would read her excerpts. Their meetings in the coffee bar were often dominated by news about Roy. Life in Canada was a bit different for Roy. He related his first visit to a pub. They had asked for his identification and as he had nothing on him, they would not serve him even though he was well over twenty-one. One of his lab mates explained the police would give the pub a problem if they found a patron without ID. Now Roy always carried identification and applied for an identification card with his photo. He also now had a Canadian driver's license which was good when challenged in a pub.

Roy was doing well in the chemistry laboratory and had made many friends. He was a teaching assistant in the laboratory and enjoying his role as a teacher. He had to take courses as well as doing research. His lab mates were a multicultural bunch consisting of one Englishman, two Canadians, two Indians and one American. They were helping him get his research going although they did not like his project.

London Ontario was not a big town and entertainment was limited. Roy had a bed sitter flat and had bought a car. His landlady was Scottish, and she liked him. He had admired her car, which was a '49 Buick. Her husband had been a worker in Detroit and had this car specially made and sprayed black. She was pleased to have an educated lodger. The university campus was male dominated but Roy was able to get a couple of dates. These dates with local girls always made him think about Maureen.

Letters were going back and forth; he couldn't get Maureen out of his mind. He was saving to go back to England for Christmas but he was really saving to see Maureen. Her letters had not suggested that she had a new boyfriend, and he was hoping she would be free when he met her again. Ann was seeing all these letters going to Maureen and she was jealous. One day she said, "No one writes to me."

Maureen's reply was that Roy was a special man and Ann had to find herself a special man. Ann was thinking that she wanted Roy; he could be her special man. She envied Maureen and that probably showed as Maureen read the letters to her.

Roy was able to book a charter flight, for the Christmas period that would allow him three weeks in England. The flight was from Toronto to London and the passengers were mainly students, so it was not a quiet flight. His parents now lived in Stourbridge so after reaching Heathrow he took a bus to Birmingham and then the train to Stourbridge. After a walk from the station he was greeted by his mother. He was only home a few minutes and left to take a train from Stourbridge Junction to Snow Hill station. He was in the coffee bar before Maureen and Ann. As they walked through the door, they gave him a big smile; now he was happy. Maureen excused herself to go to the toilet and Ann told Roy that Maureen was his. She could talk of no one else but Roy; Ann admitted she was a little jealous.

Maureen returned and Roy received a big kiss; she obviously had gone to the toilet to freshen up. After their coffee there was talk about how to go home. Roy suggested the train as Maureen could get off at Smethwick and he could carry on to Stourbridge. He was very tired as he had landed early in the morning at Heathrow. The train was crowded but that meant that he could hold Maureen all the way. Luckily when she left the train a seat became available, and he slumped into it.

The next day they all met at the coffee bar and Maureen gave him a big kiss. Ann gave Roy a knowing look. It was decided that Roy would go home with Maureen, she would change, and they could go to a restaurant. Ann was thinking that all she could look forward to was fish and chips with her mother. Arriving at Maureen's home, Roy was introduced to her mother Nora and two younger brothers. Nora was not very communicative, but the brothers were interested in Canada. Roy thought that possibly springing the restaurant dinner on Nora had upset her. He really did not know how to communicate with her.

Maureen said there was a pub within walking distance with decent grub. As they walked into the restaurant Roy spied an old mate whom he was not keen to see. This old friend came over and at length told Roy all the local news. Finally Roy said that they wished to order and that he should get lost. The man stood to his full height and said Roy's accent was crap. This was not the evening Roy had contemplated but after that episode, Maureen and Roy were able to chat. The meal was good, and they chatted mainly about Canada. Their chat was interrupted by the old friend leaving with the greeting, "Miserable evening; don't get lost."

Roy was tempted to reply by telling him to get lost again but he did not want to embarrass Maureen. Why did they meet a disagreeable old friend who was possibly jealous of Roy being with Maureen? Now he thought it best to lighten the mood; he wanted Maureen to enjoy the evening.

"Would you like to come to Canada maybe in late May when the cold weather has ended? Although I only have a bedsit I could make up a bed on the couch. If you could get three weeks' holiday, we could see some of the sights."

"Well I have to consult my diary, but the answer is positively *yes*."

Their walk to Maureen's house was very pleasurable with them arm in arm. The cuddle and kiss at the end of the walk had Roy suppressing his excitement. Roy explained he would have to see some relatives the next day but on Sunday he could borrow his father's car and take Maureen where she would like to go. Her answer was Clent Hills if it was a fine day. Sunday was a fine day and Nora's greeting was cold. Roy was wondering how he could soften Nora's attitude.

The trip to Clent Hills was a good choice as Maureen loved to sit on the top of the hill looking over Birmingham and the Black Country. It was a very clear day and lunch at the Fountain Inn was superb. Roy admitted that Canada couldn't match England for the pubs. The Fountain Inn was warm in temperature and in atmosphere. A log fire and a warm greeting by the landlord made this an enjoyable visit. As they drove to an isolated spot in the hills Maureen was all over him, but he repressed the temptation to do more than kiss and cuddle. He was afraid they might go too far and if Maureen became pregnant that could be a serious problem. He explained that Christmas Day and Boxing Day he would have to spend with his parents and relatives but after that he was free. In the evening of Christmas Eve, he joined Maureen and Ann in the coffee bar and all three went to a Chinese restaurant. Roy explained that there was a good Chinese restaurant in London Ontario, but Indian restaurants were in Toronto, a long way to go for a meal. London Ontario was small compared with Birmingham, but it had almost everything Roy needed. It was a very friendly town.

After Boxing Day he borrowed his father's car and went to pick up Maureen; Nora was visiting relatives and so Roy had to take Maureen's brothers for a drive. This was not what he had planned but everyone enjoyed a trip to Lickey Hills.

One of the twin brothers took him aside and asked, "Why don't you marry my sister?"

"Well she has not asked me yet."

Roy started to wonder why he had not asked Maureen. Nora was home when they dropped off the boys and she thanked Roy for looking after them. This was the first time he had seen Nora smile. New Year's Eve was a problem in that everywhere was booked. He borrowed his father's car and picked up Maureen. He parked the car in Holly Lane near Smethwick Junction station, and they caught the train to Snow Hill. They wandered around the city, visited a few pubs and watched the fireworks. Maureen was in a very happy mood she kept hugging Roy. Roy loved the continuous contact; it was cold, but Maureen made him feel warm.

The following days went by so fast, Maureen had to go back to work on the 2nd of January and it was back to meeting in the coffee bar. Roy was still not too keen on the bar, but it was a convenient meeting place. The day before leaving Maureen asked if Ann could come to the Indian restaurant where they had planned to have their last meal. Roy had no problem with that arrangement as he would be alone with Maureen after the meal. Maureen explained that Ann was her best friend and wanted her to say goodbye to the love of her life. Roy was a bit jealous; he had never had such a close friend. The evening went well, and Ann gave Roy a hug. The hug stirred emotions in Roy that he suppressed; he was with Maureen.

The flight back to Canada was delayed and Roy daydreamed about Maureen over a couple of beers. Back in Canada Roy found that his professor was going to transfer to the University of London. Roy had a choice to stay in Canada or go to London. This would not happen before September and not interfere with Maureen's visit. Roy had to give his reply to the situation in July, so he had time to discuss it with Maureen. He decided not to put any of this information in letters to Maureen. His plan was to wed Maureen in September in England and then either to return to

Canada or stay in London England; he had not made up his mind at this point.

May was approaching and Roy was becoming excited. At this point he had still not made up his mind about the future except that he was definitely getting married, if Maureen accepted his proposal. He had planned to take Maureen to Niagara Falls but if she was too tired, he would take her to a motel near Toronto Airport. At one of the local markets he saw a gold ring, just what he needed. He bought it and the lady asked who it was for. He told her it was for his sister, but he thought it would only fit on her little finger. The lady gave him a knowing look which he missed.

The meeting at the airport was a joyous occasion, Maureen was all over him. She said she had slept on the plane but when they were coming in to land she had a fantastic view of Toronto. They picked up the luggage and Roy asked what she would like to do. She had no idea and just wanted to be with him. On the way to Niagara Falls he realized she was tired so he pulled over so she could sleep. He then decided to find a motel and as they pulled into the car park she awoke. Roy said he had a gold ring to put on her finger, but she produced another gold ring. They both sat there laughing.

They checked into their room and when Roy came back with the luggage Maureen was asleep on the bed. Roy thought it best to let her sleep and she did all afternoon and night. Roy fell asleep and when he awoke, she was having a shower. He thought he had better give her chance to acclimatize and so he could wait until they reached London. After his shower they checked out and he took her to a diner for breakfast. This was an old-style diner which looked like an extended caravan. He ordered two bacon and eggs (over easy) and brown toast with marmalade. While they were waiting for their breakfast Maureen whispered to Roy pointing out the breakfast that was being eaten by a man at the next table.

"That looks like the full breakfast there are two eggs, bacon, sausages, tomatoes and fried bread. I think he has missed the hash browns. For afters he has pancakes with butter and probably maple syrup. I ordered the small breakfast for us."

When their order came Maureen couldn't believe this was the small breakfast. She said she couldn't eat this much food. Roy told her to eat what she could but not to be surprised if the waitress gave her a funny look when she picked up a half-eaten meal. Maureen thought the coffee was too strong, but she was used to the coffee bar coffee that Roy disliked. They reached Niagara Falls and even though the sun was shining the spray kept the conditions cool. They watched the Maid of the Mist and Roy promised they would come back and take a ride on that boat. Maureen was fascinated by the Falls but something else caught her eye.

"I have never seen so many large ladies."

"Yes, my friend calls this the fat-arse capital of Canada. Many of the visitors are middle-aged American and Canadians. If they had rationing during the war, it must have been very generous. The men often have the same problem, and everyone here seems to eat large meals."

"Now you mention it the men have a similar problem, there are some slimmer young people, but most people seem to be middle-aged. Are they here on holidays?"

"Many of them come here for holidays. Hollywood movies have attracted many of these tourists and I suppose that is why we are here."

Roy was anxious to get Maureen to London, but he had to make a few detours to let her see the countryside. Maureen was amazed that even in an industrial town Hamilton, everywhere was so clean and rubbish free. The 401 highway had very few cars compared with the M1. Roy drove through the centre of London to get to Mrs Mac's. As they came to the house the black Buick was there, and Roy parked next to it. Roy took Maureen to his flat and asked that she not fall asleep while he got the luggage. She laughed and promised to be awake when he returned with the luggage.

Now Roy was getting nervous, how should he make the first move. When he returned Maureen was in her bra and knickers; she said she was hot. That raised Roy's temperature and he went to the bathroom to put on a condom.

When he emerged Maureen said, "What are you waiting for? I thought you would ravish me."

His reply was that he had forgotten how to ravish but rape and pillage were more his style. As he undressed, Maureen said he had come prepared. Lying next to Maureen he was in heaven and then when the action started, he had to apologize for his premature ejaculation.

"We have waited a long time and the first time was not going to be ideal, but I enjoyed it and next time we should improve."

Roy thought he had been too eager, and Maureen had said the right thing, but he was disappointed in himself. Future experiences were better as they both relaxed and Maureen was starting to play a major part. They became very relaxed in each other's company. Maureen loved the sights, and one highlight was to see the Amish near Waterloo. Roy explained their way of life. This was all very foreign to Maureen. Her diary and letters to Ann were taking a lot of her spare time. Roy had to go to the university regularly but she loved her time alone. Mrs Mac entertained her with lots of stories and gave her a ride in the Buick. Roy admitted he had never ridden in the Buick. Roy told her as she had an American visa, they should visit Detroit. He would take her to Niagara Falls on the way back to Toronto airport.

They took the 401 to Windsor and then crossed the bridge to Detroit. Maureen showed her visa and Roy his driving license; there was no problem. Roy suggested that he would lock the car doors as they moved across the bridge. At the end of the bridge, they entered an area that Roy called a Mexican area and Maureen saw it looked very depressed full of rundown down houses and cars. It was dirty and compared with Windsor, it was a slum. Maureen asked Roy if they could go back to Windsor; her first impression of America was a big negative. As they entered Canada, she gave a big sigh of relief. This experience occupied at least three letters to her mother and Ann. London was so quiet and clean; she admitted she would love to live here.

On the night before her departure Roy proposed and apologized; the ring was not what he liked but was what he could afford. Maureen had no complaints and said all she wanted was Roy. He said he had decided that he would follow his professor and study in London and would Maureen be his wife and live in London? The answer was a very loud *yes*. Maureen was so excited she nearly knocked Roy off his chair. He asked Maureen to arrange a wedding in September. It should be a rather small wedding with just immediate family and of course Ann.

The trip on the *Maiden of the Mist* was very enjoyable. Maureen said that was almost as good as intercourse and then winked. Roy was unhappy they had to part and Niagara Falls was well back in his thoughts. At the airport Roy was trying to find a gift that he could give to Maureen, he decided a bottle of maple syrup with a recipe for pancakes. She was in tears when he presented it to her, this was real Canada. Maureen realized this was a holiday, but she would have loved to stay in Canada.

After Maureen went home, Roy had to concentrate on his research and plans to move to London. He had very few possessions and could give unwanted items to other graduate students.

Maureen was relating everything to Ann including very intimate details; Ann was her best friend. Maureen was not to know that Ann was visualizing a very different situation. Now that Maureen was getting married, Roy was lost to her. Roy's holiday for Maureen was so romantic it had her almost in tears.

Roy arrived at Birmingham airport to be greeted by both Maureen and Ann, who had taken the day off. Maureen was kissing him and finally he gave Ann a hug and she certainly hugged him back. They took the train to New Street station where Ann left them. Roy had quite a bit of luggage so they would need to get a taxi when they reached Stourbridge Junction. As they waited for their connection Maureen couldn't stop kissing him. She said she was making up for the months since May.

Arriving at Roy's parent's house his mother greeted them as though she had seen them in the previous week. Cups of tea, sandwiches and a slice of cake were provided. Maureen said she had to watch her figure, but Roy reminded her of Niagara Falls. Maureen had only met Roy's parents a couple of times, but the ladies acted as though they were intimate friends. Roy's father was out and did not return by the time Maureen left to go Smethwick. To get to the station they had to walk across a field with cows. Maureen was staying very close to Roy, suspiciously eying the cows, while Roy was smiling and enjoying the experience.

The welcome at Maureen's house was not so cordial but when Roy said they would be living in London, he did get a smile from Nora. The wedding plans were well advanced, and Ann was going to be a bridesmaid. Roy had picked a cousin as his best man; he thought his brother was too young. Maureen asked her brothers whether they would be page boys but they declined.

The wedding was a success with fine weather and all the relatives getting along. Nora seemed to be okay with Roy's family and Roy was pleased. The married couple went to London for a honeymoon and a chance to look for a place to live. Roy showed Maureen Queen Mary College in the East End of London where he would study. She was enjoying the Underground as she had not been to London. They of course saw the normal tourist sites and they even went into the Tower of London to see the crown jewels. Maureen was looking forward to living in London.

London rental prices were pretty steep, but they found a small furnished flat in Ilford. When Maureen got a job near to Ilford, they were comfortable. They enjoyed living in Ilford as all the necessary shopping was very close. The train service to London was frequent and they used it regularly. With Maureen earning a decent salary, they could afford to go to the West End about twice a week. They went to the theatre at least once a month and the cinema quite often. Roy found a Chinese restaurant in Slaughterhouse that was reputed to be one of the first Chinese restaurants in London; they both enjoyed Chinese food and visited this restaurant quite often. Despite all the facilities, Maureen preferred London, Ontario. She was always talking about going back to Canada where, as she said, everything was so much cleaner. Roy was also deciding that although he enjoyed London, he preferred the quiet of Canada; even Toronto seemed less hectic than London.

They visited the Midlands about every two or three months. Roy would hire a car and they would stay with Roy's parents. When they visited Maureen's mother Roy noticed a frown on Nora's face particularly when Maureen talked about going to Canada after Roy's graduation. Each time they visited Birmingham they met up with Ann; she had not met the man of her dreams.

As Roy was nearing the end of his degree, they started to think about going to Canada. Roy had an immigrant visa, and it was easy for Maureen to get a similar visa. There was a temporary position at the university in Guelph and Maureen was keen to live close to the Amish. When she told Nora of their plans there was an argument. Maureen said her mother could visit but Nora replied that she would not set foot in Canada. Roy was surprised by the intensity of the argument and he and Maureen's brothers were silent. Roy suggested that the boys might visit when they were older.

"They are not going to Canada," shouted Nora.

Maureen and Roy quickly departed and drove to Stourbridge. They were silent for a while until Maureen said, "Don't mind my mother; she will come around. I think she is possessive where I am concerned as I was born when Mom and Dad were in love. The boys came later when relations were deteriorating. My mother can be very stubborn at times; since Dad left, she has anger inside her. I still want to go to Canada, and I will no matter what my mother thinks."

Roy was trying to be conciliatory and said, "She will probably come around in time."

"It may take a crisis for her to change her mind."

Roy submitted his thesis, and it was approved. Immigration for Maureen was approved, and they were off to Canada on a liner leaving from Liverpool. Maureen was so excited.

Roy never asked about Maureen's father, he thought that she would tell him when she felt comfortable. The reception in Stourbridge was so different. Roy's father was talking about visiting Canada. Roy's mother insisted she come to Liverpool. The next morning they set off with Roy's father driving. The ladies in the back seat were enjoying the journey. When they arrived at the dock, Maureen was surprised to see the size of the liner, the *Empress of England*.

They were taking a liner from Liverpool to Montreal as Roy had done on his first trip. He was hoping there would be younger passengers on this ship. In the information package there was a card asking about the people they would like to sit with at the dining table. Roy would have Maureen by his side, so he was not worried but put 'people of a similar age'. As it turned out, the other six people were over sixty. Two couples were visiting children and one couple was going to cross Canada on the Canadian Pacific. Their meals were very pleasant as the people at the table were very friendly. The transatlantic crossing was very smooth, and they played a few games otherwise they entertained themselves. They danced a few times and lay on chairs on the deck. It was a bit chilly, so they did not spend too much time on deck. Their cabin had a porthole but the bed was the most used piece of furniture.

Sailing down the St. Lawrence was magical; there were small French Quebec villages all having churches with spires. There was an assortment of craft on the river including logging boats. At one place they saw a log raft; trunks all tied together being pulled by a small boat. The entertainment on the ship was really meant for older passengers but they enjoyed it.

They docked at Lower Quebec City which, with its wooden houses and a wooden sidewalk, reminded Maureen of Dodge City. Customs and Immigration took little time, and they took a taxi to Quebec City proper. Maureen was enchanted by this city; it felt so French. She had been to France once when she was young but now, she could appreciate the architecture and the language. Cobbled streets reminded her of some parts of Birmingham. Roy pointed out that this language was Québécoise, and it had some old French words mixed with some English words. He said "to fill my car with petrol I can ask for *'deux gallon de gas'*." He also told her that English was more acceptable here than in the French area of Montreal. They went to a café and Roy bought Maureen a flavoured coffee; it had cinnamon in it, which she loved.

Back on the ship Maureen was pleading with Roy to take her back to Quebec City someday.

"This province is so different to Ontario that it could be a different country."

"Some people in Quebec would love that. I think one day they will vote to secede. I also like Quebec and I promise one day we will return to Quebec City."

Sailing into Montreal had Maureen in raptures. This was a large city with lots of tall buildings. What impressed her was that everything was so clean and tidy. The taxi driver spoke English or French and he was African. They went to the train station to catch the train to Toronto. Maureen felt a little sad about leaving Quebec. They stayed overnight in Toronto and the next day went to Guelph by train. This was a short journey, and they were met at Guelph by a representative of the university. They were to stay in a furnished apartment on the ninth floor of one of the few high-rise buildings. Maureen was astounded by the view and the two-bedroomed flat (more often called an apartment) was much more than she had expected. The furniture was comfortable, and the bed was not too soft. Maureen was already planning some changes.

They settled into Guelph and Maureen easily got a job as a secretary—having shorthand helped. Maureen loved to go out to the local parks and have a barbeque on a Sunday. Most of the parks had electric barbeques (some were log-fired) and although alcohol was banned from the parks Roy was able to sneak in the occasional beer. Maureen was amused by the buying of alcoholic drinks. If you wanted beer you went to the Brewers Retail and filled in a form with your name and address and your choice of beer. A man went out into the back room, and it was presented to you after you had paid. The liquor store sold wine as well as liquor and they had a similar procedure. Alcoholic beverages were supposed to be consumed on the premises you had written on the order form. There were pubs but you had to produce ID to show you were over age and there was no drinking at the bar. One pub was run by English people, and they would come to the table to chat.

After about six months, a job came up at the University of Windsor. Roy took it and they moved south to Windsor. Maureen preferred Guelph but this was a permanent job after a probationary period. She loved the apartment with a good view from the balcony. Roy now had the chance to start his own research program and he could take on research students. Maureen was able to get a job in the local hospital and with her shorthand and typing skills she was covering plenty of jobs and loving it. She was meeting new people, answering the phone and typing doctor's letters. Her Dictaphone skills were also in demand. Everyone in the hospital very quickly became her friend.

Maureen was thrilled that they were close to the lakes and a few beaches. Although winter was approaching the autumn called fall was special for the leaf colours on the trees. She was keen for Roy to get a camera. Maureen could not get over the leaves changing colour as fall progressed.

They were enjoying intercourse regularly. So far, they had been practicing protective sex, but Maureen was seeing lots of babies in the hospital and that made her broody. Roy was keen that they save to get a bungalow and move out of the apartment, but he let Maureen have the decision. For several months they had regular intercourse, but Maureen did not get pregnant. Finally Roy talked to a doctor and took the test, and his sperm count was okay. Then it was Maureen's turn. She had complained occasionally of abdominal pains, but they were infrequent. The doctor examined her and sent her to the hospital for tests. One of the nurses joked that she was tired of seeing all these patients and now she wanted to be one. Maureen knew all the nurses, the technicians and most of the doctors. Roy was waiting when Maureen had a test and one of the doctors came out and took him aside.

"We are sure Maureen has ovarian cancer and it is at an advanced stage. We will have to do more tests."

Roy was fixed to his seat. He couldn't believe what he was hearing, and he had no reply.

"We think the cancer has spread to other organs and we need to keep her here for a week for more tests."

Roy felt tears trickling down his cheeks, but he was still locked in his seat. Finally he composed himself.

"Can I see her?"

"Yes of course. She is not in pain and after she has been formally admitted, you can spend time with her."

As the doctor walked away, Roy tried to compose himself. A nurse he knew walked past and greeted him. He bowed his head and wiped away his tears. As he sat there, he realized this was serious and he had to send for Nora, but would she come? What was he going to say to Maureen? Multitudes of thoughts were passing through his brain. A nurse came to escort him to Maureen's private room, and he walked as if in a trance. Maureen was sitting up in bed smiling.

"I think you should send for my mother. This may be serious."

"I am sorry love. I am lost; this is all such a shock, and I can't move mentally and even find it difficult to move physically. "

"You have to be strong for me; you were always the one who made decisions and now I need those decisions more than ever. Please be strong for me."

Now Roy was tearing up again and he couldn't hide it from Maureen.

"Roy I will take any medicine or operations they decide but you must be here for me. By the way we never did get to Quebec City."

Roy was not sure how he drove home but now he had to contact Nora. He had her neighbour's telephone number, so he gave them a message. He also sent a telegram saying *'Please come, Maureen very sick, airline tickets on way.'* He then booked a ticket from

Birmingham to Toronto and then to Windsor. Exhausted he lay on the bed and went to sleep. Roy had booked Nora's flight to Windsor as he couldn't stomach a long drive to Windsor from Toronto with Nora. The next question was would she come? It was a couple of days before he received a reply, it seemed an eternity to him.

"I feel like a fraud in this bed while there are sick people out there who need this bed."

"I am missing you; I want you in our bed."

They let Maureen out of hospital and said they would start chemotherapy during the next week. That was good timing as Nora arrived on the Saturday. Maureen was only in pain occasionally, but she was continually tired. They met Nora at the airport and mother and daughter hugged and kissed for a long time. Roy stood there watching.

"Mom, meet the best husband in the world. He bought me to this wonderful country. Showed me things I never thought I would see. I am being treated in the hospital where I work and know the doctors, nurses and all the other staff. What more could I ask?"

Roy looked at Nora and he wondered if he was blushing. Nora stared back with a sort of blank expression on her face. Mother and daughter sat in the back seat of the car and chatted all the way from the airport to the apartment. Roy left them and went back to work. He was not sure what to do or even what he could do. For Maureen's sake he had to be calm and quiet, but Nora's presence was not going to improve his mood. When he got home Nora was watching the television and Maureen was asleep in the bedroom. She awoke as soon as he entered and gave him a kiss.

"This is not going to be easy, but I must have my mom here."

"I know; that is why I sent for her. I just want you to get well and if your mother can help then she is welcome."

"When you go to England for Christmas you must contact Ann and tell her what happened; I have not written to her for a few months."

Roy had difficulty in not contradicting Maureen. They were both booked on a charter flight but that was months away. Now Maureen was saying she might not come. Roy had a lump in his throat.

"Go see Ann; I have her address in my notebook, she likes you and maybe she will be still single."

Roy felt sick. Maureen was predicting her own demise and almost telling him to find another wife. The only thing he could do was to kiss his wife; he was lost. Roy felt the next few days were like being in purgatory and then Maureen went into hospital. He could drive Nora to the hospital then go to work. In the afternoon he could relieve her and arrange transport for her to get to the apartment. In the evening he spent time with Maureen until they kicked him out. Maureen was having chemotherapy and she felt dreadful. Each time Roy saw her she looked worse than the time before; she was sinking before his eyes.

One morning, Roy got a call from the hospital. He and Nora were to come to the hospital to talk to the doctor. Roy thought this was the call he was dreading. He had to tell Nora and she was in tears before they reached the car. The doctor explained that Maureen had died in the night and by law they had to do an autopsy. Roy and Nora sat in silence. Roy should contact a funeral director so that the hospital could let him know when the body was available. Maureen had told both Nora and Roy that she wanted to be cremated. Nora wanted to see the body, but the doctor said that was not possible at present. Roy wanted to explain but the words would not come out of his mouth.

The words written on the death certificate were: *Cause of death, ovarian cancer at a very advanced stage*. Nora and Roy had to communicate, and Nora told Roy she wanted to go home as soon after the cremation as possible. Roy arranged the flight for the next day; he wanted relief and time to grieve on his own.

The ceremony was non-denominational and there was a good crowd. Roy had some friends and students from the university and the nurses and doctors were well represented. They all knew Maureen and wanted to wish her goodbye. Roy was the only one to speak;

he had asked Nora whether she would say a few words, but she declined.

"I thank you all for coming; Maureen knew you all and would be pleased to see you here. I am grief-stricken; Maureen was the best wife ever. She loved Canada and chastised me that I had not taken her back to Quebec. My mother-in-law said she couldn't speak as she would start blarting, that means she would start crying, a place I am not far from either. Tomorrow I start a new life and it is going to be a worse one than before and frankly I don't know where to start."

Roy ended his speech, and the coffin was taken into the fire while Jerry Lee Lewis, sang *Great Balls of Fire*.

Nora departed the next day and Roy had too much to drink. He decided that drinking was not going to help so he threw himself into his work. After about a week he realized the apartment was a mess. He had never been tidy but now he realized how much Maureen would do that he did not see. That put him into a depression, but exams were coming, and he had to concentrate on work. As the months passed and Christmas was approaching he started to think about what he had to do.

Roy talked to one of his colleagues who had recently lost his wife. He was an older man, but Roy respected his opinions.

"I don't really know how to grieve. When Nora left, I thought I could sit and grieve."

"No one knows how to grieve and often we do not know when it is happening. Every time you miss your wife you are grieving. When you sit alone in the evening and the silence is too much, you have to put on the radio or TV. When you go to bed and can't sleep as there is no one to cuddle. Every time you do something or make a decision and ask yourself would Maureen approve? Many men miss female company, I did. I play euchre at the club not that I really like the game but 80% of the participants are women. I am in woman's company, and I listen to their chatter, and they talk to me. I lost my wife later in life, but you are a young man you should consider marrying again if you can find the right woman."

Roy asked himself why he was going to England.

Part 2

As Christmas approached, Roy checked on his flight. It was a charter flight booked months earlier and he had to make sure it was flying. He had cancelled Maureen's ticket and confirmed his own. He would fly to Toronto and have a few days to see Toronto before his flight to Heathrow. It gave him time to pick up a couple of presents. His parents would be satisfied with anything Canadian, so it was a tablecloth, tea towels and a flag. He was not getting anything for Nora; nothing would be appreciated. Ann was the problem. A coffee mug with a map of Canada did not seem enough so he picked a tee shirt with a NativeCanadian symbol that seemed appropriate. He picked one a size bigger than Maureen and hoped it would fit.

Roy was thinking of all the things he had to do, and it was giving him a headache. He had to see Nora and give her half of Maureen's ashes; not a task he relished. Maureen's death had to be explained to his parents. They never really knew Maureen, but they needed the information and knowing them they would take it easily. Ann was the best problem-solver; he could tell her everything. Maureen had given him permission and pushed him towards Ann. He was still a bit wary he had only been a widower a few months. Maybe Ann was a bigger problem than the other two. He wondered whether it was right to try to see Ann. Maureen had given her blessing, but he was still unsure.

Landing in London, he took a bus to Birmingham and found a coach to Stourbridge. As the Stourbridge taxi pulled up at his parent's house, his mother was pruning the roses. He thought it was the wrong time of year. His mother just greeted him and asked whether he wanted a cup of tea. This was not a surprise to Roy and although she had not seen him for two years, she was greeting him as though she had seen him last week. After a cup of tea and a short chat, he had to leave.

He deposited his luggage and said he would need to go to Birmingham, and he may not be back for dinner. This did not faze his mother; she was going to make him a bed in the spare room. Striding to the station across fields he felt good. The train journey to Snow Hill was interesting, all the stations seemed to have changed. Arriving at his destination he now had to think what he would do. It was before five p.m. and so he accustomed himself with the centre of Birmingham. Just after five, he made his way to the coffee bar. In a way he hoped Ann would not be there, but she was sitting alone. As soon as he appeared before her, she smiled and gave out a quiet scream.

"I hope I did not surprise you?"

"You surprised me, but this was a pleasant surprise. Where is Maureen?"

"Maureen is dead, and I am here under instructions to tell you all. I will get a coffee and calm my nerves." Roy was not intending to be so blunt, but the words just came out.

"That is a real shock. Maureen had not written to me for a while and she was always sending more letters than I wrote back. Was it a car accident or some other accident? Maureen was always a very fit girl."

"Maureen died of ovarian cancer, it was fast, and I don't think she suffered much. She told me I had to talk to you. I am still in shock, and I am not sure what I say will be coherent but please bear with me."

As he started to recount the story, he felt he needed fresh air.

"Can we go outside and sit on a bench; I know it is cold, but I need fresh air?"

"Of course. It is a good job I have my gloves."

They sat on a bench in the churchyard and Roy continued the story. At times they were both close to tears. Finally he told Ann she had taken a real weight off his shoulders. There was nothing he could say to Nora and his parents did not know Maureen well. Ann knew Maureen before Roy and had kept in touch by mail.

"Tomorrow I have to take Maureen's ashes to Nora; a task I am dreading. I might need cheering up in the evening, can we meet at about seven p.m. and I will buy you a meal. I hope I will be good company."

"Yes please, we can meet here."

They walked to Snow Hill station and Roy left Ann at her bus stop after getting a peck on the cheek. He took the train back to Stourbridge, he felt relieved that he had taken a lot off his mind. At home his father was keen to show him off at the local pub, so Roy relaxed and had a few beers.

The next day he rode the train to Smethwick. As he approached Nora's house, he almost turned around, but he knew he had to go through with his delivery. He was almost shaking as he knocked the door. Nora opened the door said nothing but ushered Roy in with the swing of her hand. The two boys were sitting on the settee, and they just nodded to Roy. No one spoke and Roy handed Nora Maureen's ashes. She did say thank you and that was it, he was ushered to the door. He was so glad to get outside, and he walked to the nearest pub for a drink. That visit had been nerve wracking, but it was soon over. Sitting with his beer he was regretting he had never got to know Nora.

The evening meal at an Indian restaurant was a relief; he told Ann what had happened, and she was very sympathetic. She said her mother was called Vera and hoped she was not as daunting as Nora. They went to an almost empty restaurant and Roy was happy they could have a quiet chat. At one stage he apologized for talking about Maureen so much, but Ann told him to carry on. She recounted bits of his letters he had sent to Maureen, and he was amazed she could remember such detail. He decided he would spend most of his vacation with Ann, except for his parents and brother there was really no one else. He presented her with the tee shirt and the mug, and she gave him a kiss.

"Can I pick you up tomorrow night and we can go for a drink? I know your address and I can get a train to Handsworth, and then walk up Booth Street. I know the area fairly well as I had cousins who lived off Booth Street. We could walk to the Farcroft or any pub you decide."

"That would be fantastic my mother goes to bingo tomorrow night."

During the next day Roy received a phone call. It was from Mike, one of Maureen's twin brothers. He apologized for his mother's behaviour. He explained that since Maureen's death, Nora had become unbearable. She blamed Roy for taking Maureen away and then letting her die in a foreign country. He and his brother knew Maureen loved Canada and Roy, and her death was unfortunate, there were no hard feelings from them. Roy was so relieved to hear that her brothers did not blame him. He could only sympathize with his brothers in law having to suffer their mother.

The next night he found Ann's home and knocked on the door. Vera opened the door and said, "so you are the new attraction, at least you are better than the last one and that was a long time ago."

"Thank you for the compliment, Mrs Smith and I hope you win at bingo tonight."

Ann came bounding down the stairs and said, "I hope you are not being rude to Roy."

"No, I thanked your mother for her compliment."

Vera looked at Roy, frowned and left. Roy was ushered into the living room and Ann pushed him onto the settee and was all over him. She was kissing and hugging him and saying she had waited a long time. Roy told her to slow down so he could get his breath. He told her he felt a bit guilty, but he thought Maureen would want them to get together. Ann also thought Maureen knew that she wanted Roy. Maureen always had a lot of detail about Roy in her letters. She shared them freely and was not embarrassed with intimate details that some of the letters contained.

They went to the pub and had a good chat. As they walked to the railway station Roy thought that the street lighting around the station was inadequate, so he persuaded Ann to go home. She did after multiple kisses and hugs.

The next day Roy went to Ann's house, and he was greeted by Vera.

"Did you win at bingo?"

"Yes, I did."

"No need to thank me."

"No it never crossed my mind."

They both laughed and Ann was curious as to why they were laughing. When they were outside, she said her mother barely laughed so Roy must be doing something right.

In the restaurant, Roy explained his aunt and uncle would be visiting especially to see him, as they had not seen for a few years. He would have to have dinner with them and go to the pub with his uncle and dad. As compensation and as the next day was Sunday he would borrow his dad's car, pick her up and go for a drive. He asked where she would like to go, and she said Clent Hills; Roy was surprised. She said Maureen had told her it was a magical place. Roy nodded and he thought she knows a lot of detail he had almost forgotten.

Ann said she did not really know her uncles and aunts. In fact she hardly knew her sister and brothers. Her mother was always arguing with her elder sister and her elder brothers rarely visited.

On the Sunday morning he drove to Handsworth and was greeted by Vera.

"I have come to take Ann off your hands so you can have a quiet Sunday. No need to thank me."

"No it never crossed my mind."

They both started to laugh. Ann was nodding her head as they drove to Clent.

"I can hardly get a smile from my mother, and you are making her laugh. My brothers and sister will not believe it when they come for Christmas."

"Let's say I don't want the kind of relationship I had with Nora. That has scarred me for life. I generally get on with people I meet, and I don't like to put others offside. My aim is to please and so far with your mother I am succeeding."

Roy's father's Morris Minor did better in Clent Hills than his old Ford had. Walking up the hills he realized Ann was much fitter than him. Roy was surprised at his lack of fitness. He would have to lose weight when he returned to Canada and get fitter. Luckily it was a cold but clear day, and the view was as good as ever he remembered. At the top of the highest hill they sat on grass covered by a plastic sheet. Roy had expected the grass to be wet and came prepared. Ann sat very close to Roy and wrapped her arms around him. He was pointing out Birmingham and parts of the Black Country. She seemed to be looking more at him than the scenery. It was very peaceful as there seemed to no other people on this cold Sunday morning. Ann said she could see what Maureen liked about this place, but it would not be the same without Roy for company. This place was so quiet and isolated they could be intimate. Roy resisted the temptation and suggested lunch.

It was approaching noon, Roy said they could have lunch at the Fountain Inn. He had done this several times with Maureen and he was wondering whether he was retracing old steps. The inn had a roaring fire, and the meal of roast pork and apple sauce was very good. Ann had a good appetite and left a clean plate. After lunch Roy said he would drive to the

River Severn and then back to his parent's house. Ann was pleased to do anything he wished. Roy said when he was young, he was taken to Bewdley several times by a neighbour who had relatives with a bungalow on the Severn. His most vivid memory was standing on the bridge during a thunderstorm watching the lightning. He was scared stiff, but he was never afraid of lightning again. Windsor could get some spectacular storms which he could watch from his balcony. He described the view, but Ann seemed to know all about the balcony and view. Obviously, Maureen's letters had made an impression on Ann, and she was remembering a lot of detail.

They sat by the river for a while watching a couple of hardy fishermen who seemed to catch nothing while they watched. This was a peaceful place with the moving water and the rustling of the trees only providing a background sound. Ann was sitting very close to Roy and often giving him a peck on the cheek. As they drove to Stourbridge Roy warned that his uncle and dad would probably be asleep after their meal preceded by drinks down the pub. Roy asked about Ann's dad.

"My dad was killed during the war not long after I was born. My mom's parents were fairly well off and helped my mom with four children. I saw very little of my dad's parents but there were always good presents at Christmas. My mom had a pretty rough time with four children, but she is a strong woman. She has a lot of photos of my dad and us when we were young. She will not have them on show and my brothers and sister have not seen them for many years. Knowing you she might let you have a look."

"That might be very tricky ground that I will approach like a minefield. Photos often have a hidden secret, but I would love to see them."

Arriving at his parent's house they were greeted by his mother and aunt who were very wide awake. The ladies were preparing Christmas puddings and the men were asleep in the front room. Ann had to have a cup of tea and a piece of cake, a ritual for all guests. Roy just introduced Ann as a friend of Maureen. Roy showed her a photo of his brother. Ann said she thought she had seen him at the wedding.

"He is at uni and is spending Christmas and New Year with his mates. He says he will come to see me after New Year but knowing him it will be on the last day. I think he is planning to come to Canada in the summer on a limited student work visa. There is always seasonal work around Windsor. It is quite a small town surrounded by a good growing area. Knowing him he will have fixed up a cushy job somewhere."

As the next day was a working day for Ann, they excused themselves to leave early. Back in Handsworth Vera was watching TV and it was a quiz show. Roy asked what it was about and then started answering some of the questions. He asked Vera if it was okay and she said, "Go for it; the questions are too hard for me. By the way, what do you do for a living?"

"Mom, don't pry."

"That is okay," he said to her then replied to Vera, "I lecture chemistry at a university in Canada."

"Oh so you're an intellectual not some bloke in a dead-end job. I am pleased."

"Thank you for the compliment, Mrs Smith. May I call you Vera?"

"No not yet it may take a few more meetings."

"Mother you are being rude."

"No she is not; she is just being careful but now she knows I am not some ordinary bloke off the street she is happy. I will try and impress her by answering more questions."

Vera smiled; she liked Roy, but she also wanted to tease him.

The next two days were only different in that they went to the Regal cinema in Handsworth. Ann cuddled up to Roy and it reminded him of Maureen at the Princes cinema in Smethwick. Again he had no real memory of the film.

They had no plans for Christmas Eve so Roy parked outside Ann's house, and they caught the bus into town. Most eating places were fully booked but they finally found a restaurant. This time it was a Chinese restaurant, they both liked Chinese food. After the entrée, Roy asked if she would like to visit him at the end of May in Windsor. He thought she would knock the table over in her excitement.

"I want you to come to see if you could live in Canada as my wife."

"Is that a proposal?"

"No but this is. Will you marry me as long as you are willing to stay in Canada?"

"No other words come to mind except *yes, yes, yes.*"

With that she rounded the table and nearly knocked him off his chair when she gave him a hug and kisses. Some of the other patrons started clapping. Ann was almost hyperventilating she was so excited.

"Let's keep it quiet for a while and can you make arrangements to get to Toronto. You will need no cash in Canada but make sure you have some as the Canadians can get stroppy about arrivals with no cash."

"Yes, I can do everything including an American visa; I want to see Detroit. Maureen was very descriptive when she described that city. I wonder if it can be so bad."

Roy was repeating most things he had done with Maureen, but he felt comfortable this way. The only thing different was to have a rapport with Vera which he never had with Nora. To be fair he had never tried with Nora. Before delivering Ann to her house he promised to come on Boxing Day to meet Ann's family.

Christmas Day was quiet and all he could think about was Ann. He was expecting some questions about Ann, but no one mentioned her. It was lucky his brother was away as his aunt and uncle used the other bedroom and he slept in the small spare room. Christmas evening was spent with his father and uncle in the local pub. Roy drank his beer, but he was thinking he enjoyed the Canadian beer better; he kept his thoughts to himself. After lunch on Boxing Day, he borrowed his father's car and drove to Handsworth.

He was welcomed by Mike, Ann's eldest brother.

"What have you done to our mother? She is civil to everyone. This is Tom, Alice and our wives. Normally everyone is scared of our mother and when Alice meets Vera there is an automatic argument. Today everything is calm, and I heard our mother singing in the kitchen. Last Christmas was like purgatory."

"I think your mother needs a laugh now and again it can't have been easy bringing up four children. I think I should give her a hug when she appears."

"Beware she could bite but I have to see this."

As Vera appeared Roy said Merry Christmas and gave her a hug and she hugged him back with a smile on her face. The onlookers were all speechless and shocked.

"No need to thank me."

"No it never crossed my mind."

They were both having fits of laughter while the audience was spell bound.

"You can now call me Vera."

"Thank you, Mrs Smith, sorry I mean Vera."

Again there was laughter and the two men joined them, Alice was frowning. Ann appeared asking what was happening; no one could explain. Roy presented Vera with a piece of Christmas pudding his mother had sent for Vera and Ann. He explained this was only a year-old pudding as they had eaten the two-year-old yesterday.

"I used to make Christmas pudding. When did I stop?"

"Was it when they stopped putting three penny bits and sixpences in the puddings?"

"You cheeky bugger but you are probably correct."

Mike whispered to Ann not to interrupt as this banter was magic. As they sat at the table Roy finally decided to broach the difficult subject.

"I understand your husband was killed in the war. Vera, how come you never married again; you are an attractive lady?"

The other conversations stopped as Vera recoiled and said, "No other man could come close to my Jeff and who would marry a woman with four children, one of them is still at home. Jeff was a navigator and was shot down over France in 1944. Before the war he decided to train as a navigator and his grammar school education got him into a position where he was training other navigators. I always talked to him about his job, and he valued my opinion. He decided to join up as he did not want to be conscripted. I think about him often and the pain of losing the one you love lingers. I can still see his face and I don't have to look at photos. Would you like to see his photo?"

"Yes please, and photos of you when you were young."

Vera gave a laugh, nodded and went to her bedroom.

Alice asked, "Are you Rasputin or Svengali?"

Roy sat next to Vera as she showed him lots of photos. Everyone else was interested as they had not seen them for many years. Roy picked one photo of Vera and Jeff and said, "You should frame that and give copies to your children."

Vera sat back and tears came to her eyes.

"I am sorry Vera. I was being too forward, and it is none of my business."

"No you are right. I have hidden their father from them because I thought of him as mine alone and that is selfish. You have opened my eyes and now they are watering. Mike, can you make copies of this photo?"

"Certainly Mother. I am glad you asked me."

Vera was not the only one crying; everyone was crying. Roy was thinking maybe he had gone too far but Vera gave him a peck on the cheek. That lightened the mood for everyone. By the time Roy left, everyone was laughing and joking. Alice was telling Ann she was lucky to find this wizard. Mark was thanking Roy for breaking barriers that had existed for years.

Ann had to go to work after Boxing Day and so they went back to the routine of meeting in the coffee bar. Ann had already put in for leave in May. On New Year's Eve Roy drove to Vera's house and had dinner with Ann and Vera. Vera said she loved the Christmas pudding and she was going to make some for next Christmas.

"I will give you a tip. I think that pudding had Guinness as one of its ingredients."

"I will bear that in mind."

"No need to thank me."

"No it never crossed my mind."

They were both in fits of laughter when Ann asked, "What is the joke?"

"Daughter, a joke does not need to have a punch line, it is an interaction of two people who thought what they had said the first time was funny. Repeated saying of the same phrase seems to make it funnier and this is a response to different situations not the situation of the first time."

"Vera that was brilliant, your explanation will stick with me, and I might be able to use it some time."

Ann was still a bit perplexed, but her mother had an in joke with Roy and that could only be good.

After dinner they took the bus to Birmingham City Centre and enjoyed the fireworks. As they kissed Ann told Roy she wished they could be alone to make love. Roy said they should be patient and look forward to May; he had trouble trying to restrain himself. By the 2nd January, Ann was at work again and Roy was meeting his brother at Snow Hill station. At five p.m. he took his brother to meet Ann. Ken was not too impressed with the coffee bar, but Roy told him it was just a meeting place. Later they could go to any restaurant of his choice. Roy had no worries about what Ann would say, she loved any food.

Ann met Ken and they immediately hit it off. She was asking him about university and what he did over the holiday period. When she went to the toilet, Ken told Roy he was lucky he had a 'cracker'. Ken picked an Italian restaurant as there was always plenty of tasty food. Ann was complimenting Ken on his choice of restaurant. After dinner they took Ann to the bus stop, and they went to Stourbridge by train. Roy explained they would get back to have a drink with their father. Their father would take great delight down the pub in introducing his two educated sons.

The next day Ann said she loved Ken and wanted to go to university. Roy said that something could be arranged as there were plenty of part-time courses at Windsor University. Now Ann couldn't wait for May. Finally when Roy was leaving, the family, Ken and Vera met at the bus station. Vera and Ken had a good conversation with Roy's mom and dad. Roy and Ann who was in tears, were left to comfort each other.

Back in Windsor, Roy had a lot of work but still time to write a letter to Ann. Sitting peacefully on his balcony he could put his thoughts in order. Ann's return letter was full of surprises; Vera had invited Ken to come to dinner when he was in town. Vera was taking a correspondence course in sociology and was in correspondence with Ken. Alice was now trying to find a man, and Mike, Tom and their wives were regular visitors. Ann had her tickets and visas and couldn't wait till May.

As May approached, Roy had Maureen on his mind and that was good as he was keeping the flat tidy. Would Maureen approve of him and Ann doing a repeat of her visit to Canada? Maureen's visit to Canada had been perfect and she had loved every minute now he wanted to do the same for Ann. He had taken Maureen to London, but Windsor was a longer drive. He was sure Ann would love the route he chose.

They met at Toronto Airport with Ann wrapping herself around Roy. Roy was thinking what a stunner or 'cracker' as Ken had put it. When they finally unwrapped, they collected the luggage and car. They were on their way and Ann smelt good; Roy was not sure what perfume she was wearing but he liked it.

"Are you tired? If so, we can find a motel near the airport, if not we will go to Niagara Falls. By the way we will sign as Mr and Mrs."

"Look at my finger; there is the evidence. Maureen told me what to do and I will not go to sleep when we get to the motel."

Roy was now starting to wonder what Maureen had told Ann; it was bit disconcerting. He would not stay at the same motel and this one would be very close to the Falls. They checked in and when Roy bought in the luggage Ann was ready. As he undressed, he produced a condom and she said, "No need for that; I am on the pill. I started a few weeks ago and it doesn't give me headaches. Don't worry Maureen did not tell me everything."

Lovemaking was vigorous and Ann was taking the lead. After his ejaculation, Ann persisted until she was satisfied. Roy was just loving Ann's facial contortions and her body shudders. As they lay together Ann said that was worth waiting for and the next time should be soon. Roy suggested they rest, have some dinner and visit the Falls at night. Ann just lay on top of him and agreed and then fell asleep in his arms. Roy lay there with peculiar thoughts, Vera taking sociology and Ken having tea with Vera. Roy had certainly changed Ann's family.

Ann woke up and said, "Let's have a shower together but I have to wear a shower cap as I don't want to get my hair wet. "

"If I don't like it, I will look elsewhere."

"I am sure you have already looked elsewhere."

"Yes, I always followed you as we climbed the hills at Clent."

"Wow! You were looking at my bum. If I had known, I would have wiggled more,"

"Don't worry, your natural wiggle was very sexy."

In her excitement she nearly pushed Roy out of the shower. Ann was persuaded that they should go to eat and see the Falls before more one-on-one excitement. Ann said she was not very hungry and so Roy suggested they have a burger and coffee. He ordered two burgers no fries and two coffees. The waitress asked if that meant they wanted no fries? Roy explained to Ann that the burgers would be quite big, but the waitress was surprised they wanted no chips.

Ann said that Maureen had told her about the enormous meals but when the hamburgers came, her eyes opened wide.

"Is that the normal hamburger?"

"There are larger ones and if we had ordered the chips the plate would be piled high. We could have ordered a cheeseburger with pickles so we will only have the basic burger. The normal patron would follow that with a mountain of ice cream or a large slice of pie. By the way when you finish your coffee they will come and fill the cup up for free. Just eat what you can."

Ann couldn't quite finish her hamburger and Roy warned she might get a dirty look from the waitress when she collected the plate. Ann was not keen on the coffee and refused a top-up. Roy explained that this area was special for large meals as they had many American visitors. The coffee would be better when they reached home as he ground his own coffee beans.

The Falls at night were magical and with both the stationary and moving lights, Ann was mesmerized. As they walked, Ann realized her hair was getting wet by the spray.

"I should not have worn my shower cap earlier because my hair is as wet as if I had not worn it. You could have warned me, but you are a man, a gorgeous one."

"Well the cap gave me a different look, but I prefer you with wet hair. How about we have a beer? Canadian pubs are a bit different. You can take me into the Ladies and Escorts, but we have to stay seated as you won't be served at the bar. By the way do you have any identification?"

"Well I still have my passport in my bag. Surely they won't ask me to show it? I am over twenty-one."

"I think there is a possibility."

The waiter did ask Ann for her ID and he sort of thumbed through the passport. Roy motioned for her to say nothing and they received two beers. Ann quizzed Roy about what just happened.

"Firstly he has to ask someone, and you look younger than me. Watching him I realized he might not read English, or he did not know what he was looking for. Anyway if you had no ID, he would have refused to serve us both. If you finish your drink wave him away or you will get a second glass. Each place is different but when we have finished, I will wave him over and pay with a small tip. Tipping is not so common in Canada but this being Niagara Falls it is almost expected."

As they left the bar Ann said, "It was so dark in there and even though it is night it is brighter out here. Why was the bar so dark?"

"I am not sure, but I have been told some people do not want to be seen drinking in the bar. If they have had too much you just have to wait until they leave and hit the sunlight. They stagger for a while and some fall; it is quite comical"

Back at the hotel their lovemaking was not so vigorous, and Ann blamed it on the hamburger. Roy also thought she might be tired. The next day they checked out and went for breakfast. Ann said she liked egg, bacon and a bit of sausage. Roy nodded and smiled at the double entendre. Ann did eat the whole breakfast including the sausage. Roy decided they would see some small towns along the Erie coast and then head north through Bramford to Kitchener. Ann loved the scenery and, like Maureen, she remarked on how everything was so clean. Roy went to a motel he knew, where the manager assured Ann that between seven and seven thirty a.m. they would see Amish children being taken to school.

They were up early in the morning and sat at a table outdoors. They had a good view as three buggies passed with waving and smiling Amish children. Roy told Ann he had a book at home about the Amish and she would have plenty of reading material while he was at work. This area was one of his favourite places in Ontario. Ann agreed this morning was magical.

They drove for quite some distance down the 401, which was a dual carriageway for most of the way. There were parts not yet completed, which slowed down their progress to Windsor. Ann was anxious to see Windsor. As they were entering the city Ann was very excited, when they drove into the cark park, she could hardly contain herself.

"I live on the fourth floor, and we have a lift but if you carry a few bags, I will not have to make a double journey."

"I am so excited that I will carry you if you wish."

As they entered the apartment Ann dropped the bags and rushed to the balcony. She could see most of Windsor, the river and many of the large buildings in Detroit. She had heard so much about this balcony, but it was better than she had thought.

"What a view, I even see ships on the river."
"Yes this is the route from Lake Huron to Lake Erie, a lot of cargo passes up and down the Detroit River. One year on St. Patrick's Day the Mayor of Detroit made the river green."

"Surely that is a joke."

"No it is real, but we will have to wait until next year if it happens again."

"Will I be here?"

"You will if you like Canada and marry me."

Ann almost knocked Roy over in her excitement. She jumped into his arms and pushed him back onto the settee.

"We settled this on Christmas Eve."

"No that was only a temporary proposal just in case you did not like Canada and wanted to pull out."

"I love Canada but more importantly I love you. What made you think I would not love to live here with you forever?"

"Well that is settled then we marry in late September but as my wife you will need to do something."

"What is that?"

"You have to learn to drive."

"Wow! Fantastic! I always wanted to drive. You've been teasing me. You have not shown me the bedroom yet."

"First things first, there is not much food in the fridge we will have to go shopping. I know you eat everything, but you need to pick what you will eat and drink in the next few days."

The bedroom pleasure that evening was exhausting. The next day Roy went to work, and Ann wrote a letter to her mother. She said she was sitting on the balcony with a fantastic view in front of her. It was not a static scene but a moving scene as there were large ships moving along the river. Ann thought it was better than Niagara Falls. Roy had given her a pair of binoculars and she could hardly drag herself away from the scene. Yesterday she went shopping for food and saw a supermarket that seemed to have everything and things she had never seen before. Many of the fruit and vegetables were new to her. When she thought about living here it sent tingles down her spine. She said it was hard to put everything in a letter, but she would have lots of stories when she came home.

In the next week they went to Detroit and Maureen's opinion was confirmed. Ann also told Roy to do a U-turn and go back to Canada. Roy took her to Rondeau Park on Lake Erie, but she tried the water, and it was very cold. She was amazed at the facilities in the park. They had covered barbecues and plenty of seating.

They went to a beach at Grand Bend which was on Lake Huron. This was a beautiful beach, but the water was too cold. Ann loved the feeling of sand on her feet, and she tried paddling in the lake. Roy explained that the water might become bearable in July. He warned Ann about trying to get too much sun at Grand Bend; it was easy for a pale skin to get sunburnt. On their outings they stopped at many cafes, but the meals were much smaller than at Niagara.

The weeks passed very quickly, and Roy said they would fly to Toronto to spend the last few days. Ann was depressed at the thought of leaving but Roy reminded her she had a lot to do for the wedding and that raised her spirits.

Toronto was a big city and Chinatown impressed Ann. At the restaurants she tried several Chinese dishes including chicken feet which impressed Roy. They went to the theatre and saw a top-class musical and best of all was a boat ride around the harbour. This was a twilight trip with drinks and a buffet, Ann really enjoyed herself. Looking back at the city was her favourite scene. Toronto was definitely on her future to do list. She was in tears at the airport, leaving was the last thing she wanted to do.

Roy was not long alone as Ken arrived within the week. He had his introduction lectures to Canada at Niagara Falls and then caught the bus to Windsor via London. There was one other student, Ernie (Ernest) going to Windsor and Roy had a brother and friend to occupy his apartment. Ken and Ernie both commented (at length) on the size of people at Niagara. Ken and Ernie had jobs lined up at a canning factory and when they made friends of locals their nightlife was assured. Roy spent a lot of time at work but when he was alone in the evening, he was missing Ann. The boys invited him to some parties, but he declined. Ann was always in his thoughts he missed the physical side but almost as important was the banter two people engage in when together.

Ann wrote that Roy's family was invading her family. Ken before he went to Canada had found Alice a 'friend' who was Roy's cousin called Norman. They were regularly out together, and she just learned that they were planning a tour of Europe in the summer. Vera was enjoying her course and had been to a weekend retreat where students doing the same course gathered. She was the oldest student present, but everyone treated her well and the lecturer praised her knowledge. Vera was always talking about wasted years when she could have been studying for a profession.

Roy advised Ann to start the emigration process. Ann replied she was on to it and that so far, she had filled in a few forms. Ann had made arrangements for the wedding and Vera said she would pay for everything. Her mother was full of surprises but one thing she kept secret was her inheritance.

Ken worked for two and a half months and then said he wanted to see a bit more of Canada. He regretted he did not have an American visa. Roy reminded him he was going to be the best man at a wedding in late September. Roy also told Ken to visit Quebec City and Montreal. Roy gave him some money so Ken did not have to slum it.

The next few weeks passed in a flash. As Roy flew to Toronto, he was half asleep but had a vision of Maureen, she seemed to be smiling. As he opened his eyes she was gone and then he was seeing Ann. It was a strange feeling and maybe he was seeking Maureen's approval. A couple of wines with his meal on the way to Amsterdam cured any doubts. The lay-over for a flight to Birmingham had him wide awake.

On arrival at Birmingham Airport all he could see was Ann and she was in her jumping happy state. After the initial greeting he realized Vera and Alice were present. Vera came up and gave him a hug followed by a kiss. Alice did the same and said that before Roy came on to the scene, she had a totally dysfunctional family. Everyone seemed to want to talk, and Roy told them to slow down. Vera was telling him about Sociology and Alice was telling him about Norman also she was going to take a correspondence course in anthropology. Ann had to take a back seat for once. Roy realized he had a new family.

Ann's brothers and their wives were at Vera's house when they finally arrived. There was vigorous hand shaking with Mike and Tom and kisses from their wives.

Roy turned to Ann and said, "Everyone seem to be happy I am taking you away."

Ann punched him in the arm and then said sorry.

"I probably deserved that, but I have never seen such a happy bunch."

"You are correct, since I announced our wedding, they all want to help. You have united my family as never before. They can't get enough of my stories about Canada. My sister is a revelation. I always had an elder sister, but I never really knew her, now we can talk about anything. My sisters-in-law have always been unknown quantities but now I know all my nephews and nieces. My brothers are so helpful, and Mike has a computer that is useful."

Mike offered to drive Roy to his parent's house and so Roy had to break up the love fest. Mike couldn't help but praise Roy all the way to Stourbridge.

Vera and Ann had arranged everything. The wedding was in a church in Handsworth. Vera walked Ann down the aisle with a few tears. Roy was nodding approval when Ann joined him. All the families were smiling. The bride and groom stood together; Vera and Ken's mom were shedding tears.

"You do not have to say anything."

"Yes, I am speechless, but I think silent admiration is called for in this case. Now I have seen you in all your glory with or without clothes and I love what I see."

"I can't wait to get you alone; since Canada all my dreams are about you and in some of them you are very naughty."

"Let's get the reception over before I make my move."

They both laughed.

The reception was in the church hall. Ken gave a very good speech throwing in some anecdotes and stories about Canada. He also complimented Vera on her taking his advice. Roy reacquainted himself with Norman and both families had fun. Roy said they would not have a honeymoon till later in the year when he would take Ann skiing. Now Ann was crying with joy. Alice looked at Norman and he said that skiing around Christmas might be possible.

As they left from Birmingham Airport the two families were there and Roy couldn't wait to get Ann alone. Birmingham to Amsterdam was a short hop but they had a long layover. Roy bought a bottle of Champagne, and they toasted each other. Ann finally admitted she was not that keen on Champagne and so they ended up with a couple of beers. Ann could hold her booze but was soon asleep after take-off. As they came into land at Toronto, she awoke to see the city below, now she was full of beans, but Roy was tired as he had not slept.

During the flight to Windsor, Roy was napping but Ann, with a window seat, was looking at all the land below the plane. This was her new country. She loved the orderly landscape and vowed to see more of Ontario. On the drive from the airport to the apartment Ann was trying to take in the names of streets and the scenery; she was in love with Windsor.

The bedtime ritual was not as energetic as normal, but Ann was relaxed as she knew there would be a lot more in the future; Roy was pooped.

Roy told her there was no need to get a job, but she might like to be a legal secretary. He had a friend in law who had said there was a part-time course and plenty of vacancies for legal secretaries. Ann was overjoyed; she would have a university course and a potentially interesting job. Her shorthand and typing as well as the use of a Dictaphone were all assets in her getting a job. This job meant that she could take time off for her course and would learn a new profession. She still had some time to sit on the balcony and see the moving scenery.

Ann made friends easily in the office and at the hospital. Roy had taken her to the hospital to introduce her as Maureen's friend. Maureen still had a reputation about the hospital, and many of the nurses made friends with Ann. She was also learning to drive, first with Roy but then with a driving school. On her drives she loved the colours in the trees and occasionally the instructor told her to concentrate on the road. Roy changed his manual drive car to an automatic and Ann passed the test easily.

One night Roy sat down with Ann for a serious discussion. He wanted to sell the apartment and buy a three-bedroom villa. Ann said she loved the apartment and the view, but it was Roy's decision; now that she could drive it did not matter where they lived. Roy said with their combined income they would have no problem with a mortgage. While he was investigated the housing market Ann had news: she was pregnant; they had been married three months. Christmas was coming and even if there was snow Roy would not risk downhill skiing. Ann argued she was only just pregnant, and Roy persuaded her to go cross-country skiing.

Ann wrote letters to Vera and her siblings announcing the news. Roy wrote a letter to Vera asking if she would come late August, he had heard that a first-time mother might need her mother by her side. He offered to buy a ticket and Vera would need nothing while she was in Windsor. If she could stay in Windsor for five weeks that would be good as Ann was going to work till the last minute.

Vera wrote back that she could pay for her own ticket. She was a bit surprised at a son-in-law asking for her presence but because it was Roy, she was not so surprised. She was so happy that her baby was having a baby and although she had other grandchildren their mothers were not her children. This one would be 'blood of my blood' to her, as the phrase went.

There was no snow around Windsor at Christmas so they went north. Ann had never skied before but she took to it well. Roy was watching her closely in case she fell but she stayed upright for about an hour. Roy decided that was enough and when they returned to the motel, Ann agreed. She said she had aches in muscles she thought she never had. Roy was so glad she had not fallen; he was surprised that he was so protective.

Back in Windsor they cooked an enormous turkey and lots of vegetables. Roy was asking why the turkey was so big. Ann's answer was this was her first and had to be the biggest. She spent a lot of time writing letters mostly about skiing. She was wondering if Alice had forced Norman to go on a skiing holiday. Though it was cold she loved to sit on the balcony watching the world go by. Roy often had to order her off the balcony as he was worried that she would catch cold.

Winter passed and spring was cold for a while but then it started to warm up. Ann loved her job, and she was doing almost everything in the office. The law partners were very pleased with her work and particularly her Dictaphone use. The university course was easy, and she was excelling in her class. She had more knowledge in every area. No matter what the weather she would sit on the balcony during any spare hour she had.

Roy became relaxed; there had been a short period of morning sickness, but Ann handled it well. Ann had joined a group at the hospital giving information of what to expect during pregnancy. Husbands were invited to one session and a nurse asked him if he was squeamish. He answered no but then thought about the question and thought the answer should have been 'maybe'. The nurses told them that at present husbands were not allowed in the delivery room but that might change in future. Roy was hoping that future was far off.

The summer was hot, but Ann had an air-conditioned office and at home on the balcony it was very pleasant. Ann told Roy it was okay to have intercourse, but Roy was reluctant, so they had to make do with other pleasures. Roy couldn't wait till Vera arrived. Each day the bump seemed to be bigger, and he was pleading with Ann to relax and stop work.

Vera came and Roy told her he was very glad she had arrived. Ann and Vera talked all the way from the airport to the apartment. Vera's first comment was that although there was a lift, having a baby on the fourth floor was not ideal. She tempered her negativity when she saw the view from the balcony. Vera said the first flight to Amsterdam did not quite prepare her for the transatlantic flight but a couple of gin and tonics helped. The flight to Windsor was like magic she had a window seat and looked out all the way. The land was so organized and with no clouds she could see almost everything.

Roy could now relax until Ann wanted to drive around Windsor to show her mother the town. He was okay with her driving to the office, but he had to offer to drive. His offer was rejected and now he had to sit for an hour on edge until they returned. Vera was first with a comment.

"I like the city, but we only had one near miss." Roy was alarmed, and it showed on his face.

"I was only joking; my daughter is a very good driver."

Roy's concern made her love him more.

Ann continued working and Vera had lots of time to view the scenery. She had some quiet times with Roy, and she made her opinions known. They were all positive with the exception of a fourth-floor apartment with a baby. She loved the shopping. It was many years since the end of the war, but the shops here had so much more to offer. She was very active in setting up a nursery in the second bedroom and they often went shopping without Ann. Vera was very insistent on buying some items with her own money.

The waters broke and they were off to the hospital. As Roy dropped them off at the entrance, Vera said that Roy should find a place to park and leave it to her. As he entered the hospital, they were wheeling Ann to the delivery room. Vera explained they would let her in but not Roy.

"I have had four babies and never seen one come out; this will be a first."

Roy was just so glad Vera was here and so glad she had taken over. After a couple of hours Vera came out with tears in her eyes to say he had a daughter. They were cleaning up the baby and he could see her in about half an hour. Roy was so relieved, but he had to ask Vera about the birth.

"I think Ann had an easier time than I did for any of my four; she is a strong girl, and I am so proud of her. They have so much equipment available nowadays. I don't remember any of that."

Roy and Vera sat in the waiting room with arms around each other until called by the doctor. He explained they would keep mother and daughter in hospital overnight for observation. It was a smooth birth, and the doctor was very pleased. Entering the ward Roy thought Ann looked very white but the centre of attention was the baby. Roy was almost afraid to hold her since she was very small. Ann asked Roy whether he had a name and he admitted he had not thought about a name. Ann said one of the nurses was called Julie and she liked that name. Julie Ann sounded good to Roy and Vera agreed. They did not seem to be long in the ward before a nurse was ushering them out saying that mother and daughter needed rest. Roy received a good night kiss and hug from Ann who whispered that she couldn't wait to get home.

Back in the apartment Roy asked Vera if she thought Ann looked very white. Vera's response was that Ann had just undergone a stressful ordeal, but she did agree with Roy. Roy produced a bottle of Champagne to wet the baby's head. Sitting on the balcony Vera told him that she drank a lot of Champagne when she was young. Her father always had French connections and there was always wine and Champagne in the cellar. She admitted that her taste had changed a bit and like Ann, she said to finish the bottle and have a beer chaser.

Julie was a good baby and Vera said it must be Ann's breast milk. Vera postponed her return flight to England by a couple of weeks she was reluctant to leave Julie. She told Roy that Julie was blood of her blood and that gave them a special bond. Julie was such a good baby she was always smiling but some smiles may have been wind. The day Vera was leaving Ann was in tears and Roy had never seen her so emotional. He said she should come back for Julie's first birthday.

"Never mind me, these are tears of joy and next year expect me with my shoes blacked."

After Vera left Ann was keen to go back to work. Roy arranged for a typewriter so she could work from home, the law partners were very pleased. Finally they found an older lady to be a babysitter and Roy couldn't object to Ann going back to work. Roy bought a new camera as lots of photographs had to go to England. Roy was keen to save enough money for a large deposit for a house, he hated debt and the thought of owing a large amount of money frightened him.

Julie's first birthday was approaching, and Vera arrived in Windsor for the event. Julie seemed to recognize Vera and her grandmother was so happy. Ann had lots of plans about showing her mother more of Canada than the last time. Roy was preparing for a conference in Quebec City later in the year, so he asked to be excused. He had promised to take Maureen to Quebec, but it did not happen. He wanted to make sure he took Ann there.

Ann's trip involved the beach at Grand Bend, the Amish near Kitchener and of course Niagara Falls. There was going to be a lot of driving, but Roy realized Ann was a good driver and saw no problems. He asked Vera to keep an eye on Julie because she seemed to have her parents wrapped around her little finger.

"If she wants something she does not give in, and it is us that give up. I don't know any other one-year-old child but she has the way of an older child. The other day I was watching TV and she came and patted me on the cheek. I waved her away with my hand and she disappeared. A few minutes later she tapped me on the cheek and waved me away with her hand and then walked off. Not a word was said."

Vera said she would be observant, and she was looking forward to being the one in charge of Julie.

The week passed and they returned from their sightseeing tour. Vera was very impressed. She thought Niagara Falls was a bit of a disappointment, but the Amish were a delight, and she would fit them into her second sociology course.

"I agree with you; Julie has to get her own way, but one episode has me flabbergasted. We went to a restaurant for breakfast. Julie was in a sort of highchair and I was beside her. Ann was on the opposite side of the table. Ann opened the menu and Julie reached over and put her finger on the menu. Ann tried to open another page, but Julie stopped her. Julie started tapping the item with her finger. There were no illustrations, but she picked this item. I couldn't read the description and anyway it was upside down to me and Julie. I asked Ann what it was, and she said ice cream with a choice of toping. We called the waitress and Julie was tapping the item. We ordered a chocolate topping and told the waitress we would order later. Julie consumed her ice cream with most of it going in her mouth and sat there smiling. I still wonder about how she did it."

Roy now had confirmation that his daughter was different, and he and his mother-in-law were of like mind. Ann was loath to see her mother go back to England but now she had Roy to herself.

The visit to Quebec City was interesting, Ann loved Quebec. Roy had a four-day conference so they drove on the Canada side to Quebec City via Ottawa. Ann thought this the cleanest city she had ever seen. Roy thought it was sterile and took Ann across the border to Hull in Quebec. He took her to a corner store that had beer, wine and liquor for sale on a Sunday. Ann could appreciate Roy's opinion. Montreal was a big city with basically two sides: the French and English Quarters. They stayed in the French area and noticed that if they spoke English there was little response but if they tried their poor French, there was a better response.

Ann enjoyed the drive through Quebec and Roy often had to stop for photographs. Quebec City was enchanting and while Roy was at the conference, Ann and Julie took bus tours. Ann told Roy they must spend a holiday in Quebec—she loved it. Julie was very popular with the other passengers on the bus trips. The Americans especially enjoyed Ann's accent.

Roy decided to return to Windsor by travelling south of the St. Lawrence River. The journey was through Quebec until they reached the border with America. Crossing the border led them through Upper New York State to cross back into Canada at Niagara Falls. Ann was not impressed with New York State; the areas they passed through were depressing. There seemed to be some small towns that needed a paint job. There were always abandoned vehicles and lots of scrap yards. The Niagara Falls area looked so miserable compared with the Canadian side. Ann was glad to get back into Canada.

"Next time we go to Quebec we will fly and hire a car."

"Yes madam; have you asked Julie's opinion?"

They were both surprised when Julie pointed to the sky.

"This little girl knows much more than we think; we will have to be careful what we say."

When Julie's second birthday was approaching, Vera arrived. Roy picked her up from the airport and drove to the babysitter's house. Roy warned Vera that

Julie picked up almost everything so to be careful what she said as it would come back. When they arrived at the babysitter's house Vera was greeted with Nanny Fera.

Roy said, "You only need to call her nanny."

"No that is okay. I like Nanny Fera; I have never been called that before."

Julie hugged Vera and they sat in the back of the car as they drove to the apartment. Julie was keen to show Vera her toys leaving Roy to bring the luggage. He smiled as Julie was going to drag Vera around. Luckily Ann arrived as he was arranging the luggage, to get into the lift.

"I assume Julie has dragged my mother to see something."

"Yes, they have deserted me."

As they entered the apartment Julie shouted at her mother.

"Look Nanny Fera has come to see us."

Ann smiled and Vera said, "Just call me Nanny Fera."

After a small snack they sat out on the balcony with each of the adults having a beer. Julie came and tapped Vera on the knee.

"Mommy likes beer."

"She makes me sound like an alcoholic."

"You have a smart one here; I can't remember any of my children saying such things at two years old. I agree we have to be careful what we say. You know I have missed this view; can you photograph it for me so I can show it to my friends and our relatives in England?"

"You are lucky Mom; Roy has just bought a new camera for our next trip."

"I sit here and wonder what I have missed. When I was young my father told me to travel but my mother said no. She was a force in the family and of course we were in a depression. My father would tell me money was no problem, but my mother had a low opinion of foreigners. I wanted to travel the Empire, but my mother said they were all full of primitives including Canada and Australia, so I was forbidden to leave England. As I sit here if I close my eyes, I can see my mother and father; it is a very strange feeling, but it must have to do with the peace and tranquillity."

"My father was similar. He used to talk about sailing in the Pacific. He must have read Hemingway but unlike your mother, my mother only wanted what I wanted."

"As my father died not long after my birth there was only one influence, and she is sitting next to you."

They all had a good laugh.

The next day Ann, Vera and Julie went shopping Roy said he did not feel well and would stay in bed. As they entered the flat after shopping, Roy was running down the hall to the second bathroom. Ann had Julie so Vera followed him as she sensed something was wrong. Roy was vomiting in the toilet and Vera witnessed vomit like she had never seen before. It seemed to be coming out with such force it was spraying everywhere. Ann came and witnessed the last vomit before Roy sank to the floor. It was obvious that he was also defecating and then he was lying motionless on the bathroom floor. Ann screamed but Vera motioned her to keep quiet and call an ambulance. Vera started to clean the mess and tried to clean Roy. He was lying there with his eyes open, but he was unconscious. Vera and Ann couldn't lift him, so they waited for the ambulance. The ambulance men ushered them from the bathroom as there was limited space. They lifted Roy, put him on a trolley and asked Ann to follow them to the hospital. Vera was to look after Julie who had not been disturbed by the commotion.

After two hours Ann returned and told Vera they would keep him in for observation.

"What happened, Mom?"

"I don't know. He said he was feeling unwell this morning; what did he have for breakfast?"

"I don't remember. However, he is always so well; I get a touch of the flu and he gets nothing. I have never seen him sick."

"Well, he is in a good place; they can keep tabs on all his functions so go to bed, we will visit him tomorrow. Maybe he needs rest."

Ann said she couldn't sleep as she was missing the body next to her. She admitted to her mother that they had regular intercourse which they both enjoyed.

"You are lucky when I and your father had intercourse it nearly always resulted in a baby. I wish they had all been like Julie; I am now feeling cheated."

They both laughed at that remark, but it was only just too soon as Julie appeared. They all went to the hospital in a good mood and sat in the waiting room. A nurse came and asked if they would go to a conference room. Ann's reaction was that this was unusual, but the nurse said the doctor had to talk to them in private and she would be present.

They sat in the room and the doctor and nurse came in and closed the door. The doctor came right to the point. Roy had died in his sleep with a suspected brain haemorrhage. Ann gave out a scream and fainted.

"Mommy sick."

The nurse offered to take Julie out to be cared for by another nurse. When she came back, Ann had been revived with smelling salts. The doctor was explaining that they would have to do an autopsy when Ann screamed again. Vera tried to soothe her, but she seemed to only be semi-conscious.

Then Ann said, "He has left me, Mom. What shall I do?"

Vera tried to say something, but Ann repeated, "He has left me, Mom. What shall I do?"

The door opened and a cleaner was coming in, but the doctor and nurse waved him away. He knew what had happened and stayed outside the door. The doctor left and the nurse was trying to revive Ann. Vera had to get some fresh air. As she left the room, the cleaner said that he could drive them home if Ann was not capable. Vera heard what he said but she just wanted to get some fresh air.

When she returned, the nurse was sitting with Ann.

"I have been trying to talk to her but all she will say is 'he has left me Mom; what shall I do?' Mario the cleaner will drive you home as Ann is in no condition to drive. His son will pick him up from your place. I suggest you let Ann sleep if she can."

Vera showed Mario the car and he said he knew Maureen, Ann and Roy. Roy was a proper gentleman. He gave Vera his telephone number and said he would help any time he was needed. Vera then collected Julie and the nurse helped Ann to the car. She said she would stop by after her shift. Julie, Vera and Ann sat in the back of the car. Mario knew their block and said he had been in the apartment a few times. Vera thanked him as he helped them into the lift, then he asked if he could use the phone to call his son. He held Julie while Vera took Ann to the bedroom. Ann kept repeating the same phrase over and over. Julie said she liked Mario after he left.

Vera took Julie to her room.

"Mommy sick, Daddy gone."

Vera broke down.

"Nanny Fera no cry."

"Yes, Julie what is the use of crying."

Vera gave Julie a drink of milk and made tea. She took Ann a cup of tea. Ann was sobbing and still repeating the same phrase. Vera had to leave the room she couldn't hear that phrase again. The nurse arrived and advised Vera to contact the doctor Roy and Ann used. She also offered to do shopping on the next day. Vera admitted she did not know what was in the fridge. She had to make lunch and she could see what was available. She sat on the balcony with a beer and thought about Roy. He was such a nice fellow and she loved him more than her own sons. As she sat quietly on the balcony it hit her how much she would miss him.

After lunch, which Ann barely touched, Vera asked about the doctor but could get no sense out of Ann. She did find one of Roy's diaries in which he had written the address and telephone number. She phoned and made an appointment but what to do with Julie? She phoned Mario and he said he would bring his wife and she would take care of Julie. The doctor examined Ann and said she was having a nervous breakdown and it could take time for her to recover. Put in layman's terms she had lost a crutch and had to learn to walk again. His advice was to take her to England to be around family and friends and to be away from the apartment.

How was Vera going to get her to England? She had to call Alice. Mario and his wife were having great fun with Julie and Vera thought that was good as she was not able to have much fun. Mario said the family had a picnic planned on the Sunday and could they take Julie? Vera and Ann were invited. Vera said that could be a good break. The nurse did the shopping and then Vera was inundated with offers of help from Roy's workmates. Vera couldn't believe how many people were offering assistance.

Ann's employers offered help in obtaining a passport for Julie. Ann had to sign the documents and her scrawl was witnessed by a lawyer. Mario took Julie to the picnic and Vera tried to talk to Ann. She took her out on the balcony and gave her a beer but could get no sense out of Ann. Vera took her back to her room to half-eaten food and an almost full jug of water.

Mario delivered Julie and said they'd had a great time. Julie had kept all the family amused and only at one point did he and his wife have to turn away when she said, "Mommy sick, Daddy gone."

He added, "My wife knew Roy and she had to shed a few tears."

Alice and Norman were getting visas and would be there as soon as they could. Vera now had to think about packing and shutting the apartment. She was sure Ann would get better and want to come back. Vera also wanted to come back and thank everyone. She was so touched by all the help she was receiving.

Mario took Vera and Julie to the airport to meet Alice and Norman. Julie was excited she was going to meet her aunty. Vera pointed out Alice and Julie rushed into her arms.

"Aunty Arice you have come with Uncle Orman."

Alice gave her a kiss and looked at her mother with tears in her eyes. Norman picked up Julie and asked if she liked the airport. He was trying to make some time for Alice and her mother to greet each other. Julie took Norman to the window and with her arms showed him how the planes took off.

"She is only two and she has charmed both of us and I like Arice. Now for the serious part, where is Ann?"

"She is with Mario's wife; he is not just a driver, he is also a friend."

They were transported to the apartment and Mario's wife apologised. She said Roy and Ann had screamed. Vera said that was good she still recognised his name. Vera was wondering how long this could last. Alice went to the bedroom and sat with Ann. Norman was enjoying the view and Vera offered him and Mario a beer. Mario declined and said Vera should call him any time she needed help. Julie was pulling Norman along to show him her room.

Vera relaxed until Alice reappeared. Alice was upbeat, saying she thought that Ann would change. Vera told her every time she heard that phrase it gave her pain. Alice said that with Ann the expression did not contain 'Mom' so there was some recognition that Alice was different.

Norman came back to the balcony and said, "That is some two-year-old! I have been entertained for at least an hour."

He then started to admire the view. Alice asked whether they should call Julie to eat. Vera said that when she was ready, she would appear and discuss what she wanted to eat. It was like discussing things with an adult and they would come to a compromise. She would tell Nanny Fera if she liked it or not.

"I know she is too young to know what is going on, but she wants to live her life her way."

They sat on the balcony until Julie came out and said, "Sandwich, cheese and tomato."

"Do you want any sauce or pickle?"

"Maybe onion."

Alice and Norman watched in amazement. Vera made the sandwich; Julie ate it said thank you and went to her room.

"Relax, she will be out for a drink in a minute; this little girl has a routine."

Julie appeared and asked for a drink. She then went to Alice and said, "Make my mommy better."

Alice was hiding her tears until Julie left and then she sobbed on Norman's shoulder.

The next day as they were packing, Vera found Roy's camera. She was very insistent that this should go to England. Alice asked Julie to pick her best toys. She watched as Julie put some toys on one side then started to change the sides. Alice was silent but enjoying Julie making choices.

"Mom, were any of us like Julie?"

"No, Julie is special; of course, I am prejudiced but this girl is a one-off. I think you were all quiet children and never gave me a problem, but I never had to negotiate with you. There is so much of Roy in Julie, every time I see her, I think of him."

"That is good, Mom. She will grow up and one day she will know how her father transformed our family."

As they packed, Ann came from her room and watched. Julie hugged her and Ann hugged back. Vera was watching this with a mixture of sadness and hope.

Alice said, "Let's get her home. She will get better and then she can come back here; I would."

Vera replied, "So would I."

Part 3

Vera, Julie, Alice and Norman were taking Ann home to England. The flight to England was very quiet except for Julie, who was so excited. She told the stewardess that Mommy was sick but Nanny Fera was in charge. Alice and Norman were watching and laughing. Vera ordered a wine and Julie ordered a beer for her mother. The stewardess was laughing, and Alice said this little girl was an exceptional girl. Ann sat almost motionless although she drank her beer at the urging of her daughter. At Amsterdam Airport, they sat in the lounge with Ann motionless staring into the distance. Julie was the only lively one showing Norman how the planes took off from this new airport.

Mike and Tom met them at Birmingham Airport. Ann showed no recognition of who they were even though they both kissed her. She seemed to look straight through them.

Mike took Vera on one side and said, "What can we do?"

"I am not sure; we need to give her time."

Julie was entertaining them, and Tom said none of his children was anything like Julie and Mike agreed she was special. Vera showed her the bedroom and said they would both sleep in that room.

"Nanny Fera, you snore."

Vera had to leave the room and go outside to have a good laugh. Tom asked what she was laughing at and when Vera told him he also had a good laugh.

"She is two, I can't imagine what she will be like when she is three. I really do not want her to grow up because she is so entertaining now. I have to take care of her till Ann gets well but will I be able to let go?"

Alice was going to take care of Ann and Vera was going to take care of Julie.

Weeks became months and Ann did not change. She said nothing, and the only real interaction she had was with Julie. They would kiss and hug but not a word was spoken. Vera visited her doctor, but his advice was to give her time. He could prescribe pills but unless she became violent there was not much he could do. Alice was trying her best but getting frustrated that her questions or gestures elicited no response.

One day Ken contacted Vera. He had graduated and wanted to see his niece and sister-in-law. Vera was very happy for him to visit; in fact, she could not wait. Ken came and Vera and Alice had a discussion around the table before he saw Ann. As he entered the bedroom, Alice saw a weak smile from Ann. Ken kissed Ann and she kissed him back. Then he told her he was not Roy and she nodded yes but did not speak.

He asked her a few questions, but the replies were only a shake of the head. Before he left, they had a long hug.

Alice was so excited to notice that Ken had got a greater response than anyone else and Ann was answering questions. Ken said he was out of his depth, but he thought Ann needed a stimulus; maybe he was a minor one. The only thing he could think of was the coffee bar. He had been there and hated it but that was where Roy and Ann had met. Alice thought that a good idea and said she would go look for the coffee bar and take Ann there. Ken's only other suggestion was to ask Julie to ask her mother questions. Vera bought out a very old bottle of French wine and they consumed the whole bottle.

Alice went to Temple Row and could not find the coffee bar. Now she was wondering what to do but she decided to let Ann show her where it was. The next day she took Ann to the city. Ann did not change until they arrived behind the cathedral. She looked all along Temple Row and finally said, "No coffee bar."

Alice said nothing and directed her to a bench in the church yard where Ann began to sob. Alice was not sure what to do when Ann put her hand on the seat on her side. "No Roy." Then Ann burst into tears again. Alice tried to comfort her but that was the last word Ann uttered. At home Alice told Vera and they were hoping this was the breakthrough. They then told

Julie to talk to her mother; they did not tell her what to say but they told her Ann was improving.

Julie greeted her mother and asked, "Mommy getting better?"

Ann replied, "Not yet," and Vera and Alice were smiling. Julie showed her mother a teddy bear Norman had brought her and that produced a smile from her mother. Vera and Alice were so happy.

After that meeting Alice and Vera agreed that Ken was like his brother, he did positive things for this family. They asked Ken to come back and see them as soon as possible.

Ken was looking for a job and applying to immigrate to Canada. He had loved Canada when he went on a student work visa. He was doing a Master's in Sociology and was looking for jobs in Canada. He took a weekend off from his studies and borrowed his father's car. He decided to take Vera and Ann to Clent Hills. Roy had told him that this was a magical place. Alice, Norman and Julie followed in their car. Ken parked and they walked to the top of the hill. Suddenly Ann became excited; Ken said they should look at the view. He put his arms around Ann, and she relaxed on his shoulder. Alice and Vera were so happy that they were crying quietly. Julie piped up and asked questions about the view. Ken asked Ann if what Julie pointed out was the Black Country and Ann nodded that it was. Then Ken asked Ann where they should go. Ann answered the Fountain Inn.

They went and sat by the fire; Vera said it was her treat and would not allow anyone else to pay. Ann ate steak and chips and drank one beer. Alice said to Norman that Ken's family must have a hold over her family. His answer was that they must come to this pub again; he wondered why he had not found it before.

Back home Ken said, "No need to thank me."

"No it never crossed my mind."

They both started to laugh, and Ann was smiling. Alice asked what they were laughing at. Ken explained that Roy had told him the story and he remembered the words. Roy had a bad experience with his first mother-in-law, so he decided that his next one had to be friendly, so he used that expression to lighten the mood. Ann had asked her mother the same question and Vera had explained their joke.

All the time Ken was explaining, Ann was nodding approval. Ken told Vera to put on some music as he wanted to dance with Ann. He told Ann they would dance and took hold of her. She did not object and danced a waltz to the music. Julie joined in and Vera and Alice were crying. Ken then said he would pick up Julie and then dance with Ann. Vera had to leave the room. Ken told Julie her mother was beautiful and did she agree.

Julie added, "Better before."

Ann responded by starting to cry. Ken told her that she should try to get back to her beautiful self. He was going to Canada and hoped to see her there.

After Ann left for her bedroom and Julie went to sleep, the adults sat and discussed the afternoon's events. Ken said that he was applying for jobs in Canada because his brother had decided to live there. He was young when he visited but never appreciated Windsor. Canadians were so easy-going and he decided he wanted to live in a less confrontational society. Vera said she loved the flat in Windsor but more importantly she wanted to thank the people who had so kindly offered help. Alice could not believe the impression that Windsor had on her she had only been there a few days.

After a few days, Ann started to speak, firstly with Julie. Alice could not get answers and Vera was afraid to try. Then one morning Ann came to breakfast and apologised for the last several months. Ann could not explain what had happened, but said it was like being in an empty room alone. She could not talk and there was no one to listen. The shock of Roy's death had locked her away. Later she could see visions of Roy then Maureen, these always made her cry. Julie was there but she could not understand. Seeing Ken was like seeing Roy and then the room seemed to get bigger, but she could not get out. Dancing with Ken seemed like a door had been opened. She was afraid to leave the room until she finally had to try. Now she felt very tired and decided to go back to bed.

When Ann left the room Julie said, "Mommy funny."

Vera was speechless but Alice said, "This is the start of her getting better."

The next day Vera was talking to Alice.

"Julie asked me about Canada. I tried to explain, then Julie said she and Vera could go to Canada. I told her we had to wait for her mother to get properly well. She said her mother had Aunty Arice and we could go alone. I said I had to get a visa and then had to tell her about visas. I finally told her I would get the visa forms and that seemed to satisfy her. Sometimes dealing with Julie is exhausting. She now calls me Vera; I like Nanny Fera, but she still calls you Arice."

"I think Ken and Julie had the breakthrough with Ann. I seemed to make no impression and I think that is because growing up we had little interaction. I want children of my own and that has to be soon. I am going to put pressure on Norman."

"You'll be lucky to get one like Julie, but I shake my head when I think of having two Julies."

There was a continual improvement in Ann, but she would still have periods when she went quiet and stared into the distance. Ken visited to tell them he had a job with the Canadian Government and was going to Ottawa. Ann was all over him kissing and hugging.

"I am Ken, not Roy."

"I know but I can close my eyes."

This was the old Ann, and Alice and Vera had wide grins.

Julie said, "Uncle Ken is good for my mommy."

All the adults agreed. Vera took Ken on one side and said quietly so Julie could not hear, "I think we will be in Windsor soon please let us know your address."

"I am part of this family, and I would love to visit Windsor again and I look forward to the greeting Ann is giving me."

"If I close my eyes I could be talking to Roy. After my husband he was my second love, male of course."

A few weeks passed and Vera was planning their trip to Canada. Alice said she could not go as she was planning her wedding and surprise, surprise, she thought she was pregnant. Vera was thinking that any problem with Ann she would have to deal with but maybe Mario could take Julie off her hands. Ken was writing that he would be stationed in Toronto and would be able to visit Windsor. Vera asked Ann about the trip and whether it was a bit soon. Ann answered that she really wanted to go to the flat and would try her best during the journey. Julie was so excited when Vera told her she had her visa. Mike and Tom were questioning whether it was too soon, but Vera was anxious to get to Canada.

Each day Vera talked to Ann and gained confidence that the planned trip would be OKAY. Mike and Tom were now able to talk to Ann and she seemed back to normal. Alice was the only one a bit worried, but she had told Norman if there was a problem, she would be off to Canada. Vera looked at her old photos and wished her husband could experience these developments. She knew he would have good advice. Vera was now living a new life and loving it.

The whole family was at Birmingham Airport to see Vera, Ann and Julie start their journey to Canada. There were lots of tears and also lots of laughter. Julie was so excited but disappointed the first flight was so short. In Amsterdam airport she ordered a beer for her mother and a gin and tonic for her grandmother. The waitress looked at Vera and was told this little girl had a good memory. Ann told Vera that she was anxious about this new flight; that was not what Vera wanted to hear.

The flight to Toronto was smooth and Julie slept most of the way and Ann and Vera had a little small talk. Ann was relaxed but Vera was up tight. Vera was thinking what she would do if Ann reverted to her previous state. That did not happen and at the immigration Ann took control, she now became a legal secretary. Vera was watching and was so happy that Ann was back to normal. The flight to Windsor was smooth and with Julie sitting in the window seat full of commentary. Vera had let Mario know they were coming, and he was at the airport to pick them up. He said his wife could not wait to see Julie again.

On entering the flat, Ann went very quiet; Vera was expecting the worst.

Ann said, "Don't be afraid, Mom. Give me a little time."

Julie rushed to her room and gave a shriek of joy. That stirred Ann and she went to the balcony smiling and laughing at the view. Vera asked whether she was OKAY. Mario stood motionless watching this drama.

Ann turned and gave Vera and Mario a hug and said, "I am back, and the view is as good as before. Roy wanted to get another place, but I am staying here. There are so many memories here and the view is unbeatable."

Mario said his wife had cooked dinner and they should come back to his house. Vera was a bit reluctant, but Ann was all for it. This was the Ann of old. Julie wanted to take one of her toys and was very happy to go with Mario. Augustina, Mario's wife, was so glad to see them particularly Julie. Julie recognised her immediately and ran to her to give her a kiss and a hug. Mario said his wife was very sentimental and was holding back tears. After the meal and a couple of beers Vera said they should leave as they had had a long day. She quietly told Mario she did not want Ann to have much stress. Mario understood and said if there was any problem with the car next day to call and his son would fix any problem. Vera said she was very happy to have Mario as a friend.

"I knew Maureen and Roy, they were special people, then Ann joined Roy and my feelings did not change. Now I have met Ann's mother and you make my friendship bigger."

The next day Ann went to the car, and it started first time. They had to go to the bank and Ann was welcomed by the tellers. Vera was amazed at the reception. The supermarket was the first stop, and the Brewers retail was an important second stop. Ann said they would deliver the groceries and the beer then she would go to the Liquor store. Ann was really enjoying herself. Julie was also enjoying herself telling her mother not to forget the ice cream. Lunch and a small dinner had Ann and Vera sitting on the balcony with a couple of beers, Julie was asleep.

"What next?"

"Tomorrow I will go to see if I have job, if not I will be job hunting. I want to give some money to the university for a student scholarship in Roy's name. I also want to donate something to the hospital and of course I must owe you some money."

"I think you are doing something great, but I will not take any of your money. Make sure you save money for Julie as she is such an intelligent girl."

With that thought in mind they retired to bed.

There was no problem with the job, Ann was welcomed back. The partners admitted her skill had been sorely missed. She returned to the apartment to find Julie telling Vera what she should do.

"I am wondering. Who is the adult? This little girl has a list of instructions, and I can't find fault with any of them, but I want to say no but I can't."

"Mom, I now have a job but what will I do when you leave?"

"Let's talk to Mario."

"When nanny Vera leaves my wife will take Julie at no charge. My wife and I have grandchildren but my wife likes Julie more. I have two sons who do not listen to me but when Julie speaks, I see them listening."

That was settled and now Vera could relax. She wanted to get home but was still worried about Ann. Would some vision or situation set Ann back? There was a short time before Vera had to leave but she saw Ann improving all the time. Her work was giving her confidence and she was renewing old friendships. Julie was happy to be with Augustina and Vera could leave with minimal fears.

Several months passed and everything was going well. The news from Vera was that Ken had transferred to the Ontario Government and initially would stay in Toronto but may be able to move to Windsor. Ann was excited with that news as she would have family near, and it would be Ken. She contacted Ken and decided to visit him in Toronto. Augustina and Mario were only too glad to have Julie over the weekend and a few days more.

Ken picked Ann up at the airport and asked Ann what she would like to do.

"The first time I was in Toronto, Roy and I had a cruise on the harbour with dinner and drinks, it was magical."

"Well let's see if we can book a similar cruise."

They booked the cruise, had lunch near the harbour and went back to Ken's flat to change. The flat was a small one bedroomed flat near Yonge Street, not far from the waterfront. Ken excused his flat for being poorly furnished, but he was hoping to move to Windsor in the near future. Good news for Ann who wanted Ken to be close. The cruise was a success and Ann loved the food and drinks: she enjoyed every minute. Back in Ken's flat they were getting ready for bed.

"Don't sleep on the couch; come sleep with me. I see you have a double bed."

Ken was speechless. He did not know how to react.

"We are both single adults and I miss having someone in bed with me. I miss the intimacy Roy and I had. I want you to come because you are you, not Roy."

"You are an attractive woman, but you are my sister-in-law, and I am confused."

"Please come to bed with me, I need you."

In bed Ann was all over Ken and he responded and forgot his inhibitions. Both Ken and Ann enjoyed the bedroom pleasures, and in the morning, they were refreshed to go again. The next four days, were a total pleasure for Ann. Ken was so surprised how relaxed he was with Ann. In the back of his mind, he was thinking of Roy, but he imagined Roy would approve. They discussed Ann's breakdown, and she told him that when they had danced it seemed to take her out of her spell. She admitted that pressed up against a man had a wonderful effect.

Ken wanted to talk about Roy and Ann was very willing to tell him things he would never have known. She related how she was jealous of Maureen and loved Roy from the first. Maureen's death was a big surprise, but she believed Maureen had sent Roy to her. She loved Canada from the first time she visited but not only because of Roy's presence.

Ann was very unhappy to leave Toronto and Ken said he would visit Windsor in the near future, to look for an office. He had convinced his superiors that the very southern tip of Ontario was a place to have a presence. The local Windsor MP had been contacted and he was very enthusiastic. Ken was studying how people lived and what they wanted. He was also studying things they did not want.

Back in Windsor Julie was very happy to see her mother and asked about Uncle Ken. She remembered dancing with him. That brought a tear to Ann's eye.

Ann was looking forward to having Ken in her flat and his warm body next to her.

Mario said Julie had entertained the whole family with stories about England. She told very good stories and several of his relatives wanted to visit England. Julie was not afraid of an audience. Ann thanked him and his wife for looking after Julie. She told him she had seen a lot of Toronto and she might go back in the future. Mario admitted they had passed through Toronto on the way to Windsor but had seen nothing of the city.

Ann was enjoying work and was studying to be a legal clerk. In the part-time classes, she was the oldest student, but she had much more knowledge than her fellow students. She visited the hospital regularly and renewed old friendships. Everyone remembered Maureen and Roy and she was the living link. Her doctor examined her and asked about her breakdown, as he was the one who had suggested taking her back to England. She related the whole story and hoped her information would help if he came across a similar case. He thanked her and told her he had learned information he did not have previously.

Ken visited for a couple of days to investigate his new office. This was two days of pleasure for Ann. Ken had rented an apartment although Ann said there was no need, but she thought it could have some benefits. Ken had to go back to Toronto to settle his affairs and ship his effects. Ann could not wait for him to return. When she was with him, she felt she was floating on air, nothing bothered her.

Ken returned and they resumed their intimacy, generally at his apartment. Ann was enjoying life and at a barbeque put on by Mario she took Ken, and it was obvious they were a couple. Ann approached Mario and asked what he would think if she married Ken. He was a good friend, and she was sounding him out. He thought for a minute.

"In my tradition a widow should be taken care of by the family. If my brother died, I would take care of his wife although I would not marry her. In your case I think it a good idea."

"Thank you, Mario; he has not asked to marry me, but it is good to get your opinion."

Mario was so delighted and when he discussed it with Augustina, he stressed Julie needed a father. Augustina said the most important point was that Ann needed a husband.

A few months passed and Julie's birthday was approaching, and Vera was planning to be in Windsor. She had not missed a birthday and she was not going to miss this one. On arrival she was met at the airport and Julie rushed to meet her grandmother. After a lot of hugging and kissing Julie said, "Uncle Ken is going to be my new Daddy."

Vera was stunned and she looked towards Ann who nodded in the positive.

Back in Ann's apartment Vera waited till Julie had gone to bed and Ken had left.

"Is marriage to Ken for real?"

"Yes mother, Ken and I are meant to be together, he is not Roy, but he is the one I love. I made the first move, and you should have seen his face. I think I bullied him into going to bed with me. It is an old tradition that brothers take of care of their brother's widows. Ken takes care of me every day."

"I am not sure what to say but this is outside my vision of normality. Will you let me discuss this with Ken on my own? I like and respect Ken, but I want to know his feelings."

"Before you do let me propose marriage as he has not proposed yet, Julie jumped the gun."

Vera was perplexed but realised that Julie had given her a problem, nothing new!

"Will you marry me?"

"Is that a suggestion or a proposal or a command or something else that does not come into my mind?"

"Of course it is a proposal, and if you say yes you have to talk to my mother."

"I like to talk to your mother, so I guess the answer is Yes."

Ann rushed him nearly knocking him over and was kissing him passionately. They had not noticed Julie who started to clap. Ken invited her to come and kiss him and she was happy to do so. Vera came in from the balcony to see the happy scene.

"I suppose I can have some time alone with Ken."

Julie said you can if you give him a kiss. Vera had to laugh; she had received another instruction from Julie. Vera gave Ken a kiss on the cheek and told him she was doing this because of instructions from Julie. Ken's answer was that he would thank Julie later. Julie had spoilt the no need to thank me phrase.

"Oh, you are so like your brother, but we need to have a serious discussion."

"Yes, I also want to know your views."

"When Ann told me you wanted to get married, I was shocked. I suppose it had never crossed my mind and it was foreign to me. I loved both you and Roy but both of you being married to my daughter is bizarre. Ann has explained how brothers would take care of their widowed sister-in-laws, but that was in the past and times have changed."

"I can understand how you feel. Initially it was strange to me. When I saw Ann having a nervous breakdown, I knew I had to help. I had known Ann as a very happy vibrant person, and I knew nothing about nervous breakdowns. I went away and did a lot of reading about the condition, not much of it was any good. When I asked her to dance it was a spur of the moment decision, but she responded. Maybe that was the time I fell in love with her. The meeting in Toronto was a surprise but after my initial reluctance it felt natural. I love Julie and I think she needs a father. I want to give her the best education possible because at this early age she is inspiring."

"Well, I cannot argue with that, and you are both adults. Have you thought about having children, Ann is not too old."

"I think that is a bigger question than getting married."

They went to England to be married. Ken had a long talk to his parents who were initially against the marriage. Alice said that Roy and Ken had done so much for her family she would welcome Ken as a real part of the family. Mike and Tom were against the marriage, but Vera bullied them into accepting it. Julie was a bridesmaid and loved every minute. At the reception there were a few speeches. Julie told Vera she would make one.

Pointing at Ken Julie said, "I used to call him Uncle Ken and now I call him daddy because I love him, and Mommy does too."

Escape

Tom left school at 15 just as WWII started. He became an apprentice at a local factory He was an apprentice turner and fitter which meant he was used to fill in when other workers were sick and help when machines needed fixing. He was a very capable worker and took on many jobs when other workers were conscripted. Tom was popular with the older hands as he was always willing and quite strong for his age. He knew all the problems with the machines, and he could keep production going and so was popular with management.

Marilyn joined the company at 15, two years after Tom started work. She was employed in the office as a typist in a typing pool. She had to attend typing school once a week which she enjoyed. Along with typing lessons she was also taking shorthand and was promised a raise when she completed her course. Like most typing pools there was a lot of gossip, but Marilyn was the quietest girl in this pool. She had no gossip to spread but listened to a lot.

When the bombing raids started the company built a bomb shelter on the edge of the factory compound. The managers realized their best asset was the work force. Although the factory was on the edge of Birmingham and a bit removed from other factories, it was obviously a factory. All factories were targets for German Bombers. The management was in constant communication with the home guard and would get prior warning of any raids. They were very keen to keep their workforce safe and broken machinery could generally be fixed. Tom's major job during this time was fixing damaged machinery. He loved this work, but he was always hoping the Germans would miss.

Tom was a bit of an outsider; he did not drink beer. Any celebration would send his work mates to the pub. Tom had tried beer and hated it. He would often go to the pub but would only drink pop. They teased him unmercifully, but he would only drink pop. He was offered wine and whisky but would only drink pop. In the end they gave up, but he was still made to pay his round.

During one bombing raid Tom went to the shelter and sat next to this pretty young girl. They chatted for a while and Tom found that Marilyn lived close to the factory, and he lived close to the factory only in the opposite direction. Tom determined to sit near Marilyn during the next bombing raid. The German bombers were tending to come during the night, and it was a long time before a daytime bombing raid. Tom felt guilty that he wanted a bombing raid during the day.

In the air raid shelter at the next meeting Marilyn told him about her life. This was prompted when he asked her if she wanted to go to the pictures. She said after work she had to go straight home and was not allowed out. When not at work she only went shopping occasionally with her parents, her father was very strict. She spent most of her time in the house. Tom could not believe what he was hearing. This was long raid and they talked for a while. The raid ended and Tom determined he would hear more of this story during the dinner (lunch) breaks. He would go to the typing pool and take Marilyn for a walk.

Marilyn recounted that her father became very possessive as she was growing up. In the park if other people came close, he would either shoo them away or they would leave. She once saw him hit her mother and her father told Marilyn that could happen to her if she disobeyed him. She looked at her mother, but she did not cry. There was a ritual and every Friday she had to give her father her pay packet and he would buy any clothes she needed. Tom was totally amazed at these revelations. He could not believe a grown working girl could live under such a strict regime.

Marilyn told Tom that she knew it was wrong, but she had cheated her father. When she completed her shorthand course, she received a raise. She had opened her pay packet and removed the raise. When she handed over the packet, her father asked why it was open. She told him someone had complained their wages were short. Now they had to count their wages and sign for them. Her father accepted that explanation. She was pleased with this deception.

"What do you do with your savings?" "I keep them in my desk."

"I think you should open a bank account. I will investigate what you need to open an account. Make sure no one goes in your desk."

Tom determined that as Marilyn was sixteen, she could open a simple savings account without her parent's permission. The banks were encouraging everyone to save during the war. All she needed was identification. Luckily, she had kept her birth certificate which she had used to get her job. She had not given it back to her mother. On the application she put Tom's address so nothing would come to her home. She kept her bank book In her desk at work and visited the bank every month to deposit a small amount of money.

Tom spent many a dinner time with Marilyn and they occasionally kissed. Marilyn was a bit shy about telling her office mates anything except saying she liked Tom. The meetings had to stop as Tom was called up. He and the company had applied for an exemption but that had failed. On his last Friday he decided to accompany Marilyn home, he wanted to meet her father. Marilyn thought it was a bad idea and it turned out to be so. Her father was at the gate waiting for Marilyn and his pay packet. He went into a rage and threatened Tom. Tom told him he only walked with Marilyn as they were going in the same direction. It would not happen again as he was joining the army on Monday. Now Tom knew what kind of man Marilyn's father was. The anger in that man's face had frightened him. All the way home he saw that horrible face.

Tom joined the army and almost hated every minute. He was sent to a transport unit and given an ill-fitting uniform and shown how to fold his gear. Inspection was every morning, and he was amazed how trivial mistakes produced so much verbal assault. This was going to be a long-time punishment with no sight of an end. One thing they did for him was to teach him how to drive a lorry. He was not sure how he was accepted into a transport division; maybe it was his technical skills. Tom had excelled on the firing range, and he was hoping not to shoot at another man. The sergeant complimented him on his score and hoped some German would feel the effect. Tom had no such feelings.

After about one month training and driving around the English countryside they were off to Egypt. Tom asked the sergeant what they would do in Egypt. "Drive."

"Don't they drive on the opposite side of the road?"

"Who cares, we will be in a convoy, and it does not matter which side of the road they drive, they will have to give way. Anyway I am not sure they have roads. I am told we will dock at Port Said and then drive to Cairo. I hope it is a short drive as I am told it is hot there."

Tom was training with one of the motor mechanics who showed him how to fix lorry engines. Compared with his work in the factory it was dirty work. These engines were dirty, greasy and oily and Tom was not used to working in such conditions. The journey to Port Said was a lazy time except for inspections and drill on the ship's deck.

When they reached Port Said he was one of the squad that had to fill the unloaded lorries with oil and petrol. The fumes gave him a headache, but the sergeant would not have him call in sick. Several times he had to walk away as the fumes were making him dizzy. He was so glad when this refuelling was finished. There was no time to relax as they were off to Cairo.

Convoy driving was boring, you had to stay alert as the truck in front was very close. Tom saw very little of Egypt on his first drive. After so much concentration and the fuel fumes he had a headache. When they reached the camp on the outskirts of Cairo all he wanted to do was eat and sleep. He was also very thirsty. He did not drink beer, so he slaked his thirst with water. Most of his colleagues got very drunk by consuming beer after beer.

The next morning they were mustered, and Tom was the only one without a hangover. He had to supervise some locals loading the lorries. The sergeant major was also the worst for wear and so Tom was in charge. It was back on the road but this time to Suez at the other end of the Suez Canal. It was hot and Tom was drinking water every mile. He was surprised he did not want to piss. When they arrived at Suez they were instructed to unload and wait for instructions. Locals did the unloading; Tom was very happy they did as the heat was almost unbearable. Two days in Suez and they were off to Port Said. His mates were consuming lots of beer and a few other drinks. As the lorries were unladen they left more space in the convoy and Tom saw the Suez Canal in action. It was amazing.

Watching large ships going through the desert had Tom very excited. He vowed to be on one of those boats one day. At Port Said they sat around for a few days and then were told the lorries would board a ship: destination unknown. The problem for Tom was that the lorries had to be drained of oil and petrol. It turned out that the procedure was not as bad as when the lorries were refuelled.

The other drivers were holding a sweep and four destinations were the favourites, Sicily, Southern Italy, Alexandria and Greece. Malta and Cypress were outsiders. Although Tom was not a gambling man, he drew Italy and won the sweep. Tom wrote a couple of letters to Marilyn, but he could not say much except that he loved her. She treasured those letters; she had never previously received a personal letter.

Landing in the southern tip of Italy was quite an experience. Tom was expecting some opposition from the Italians and maybe some German Bombers would hit them. The locals were very friendly, and the German aircraft obviously had other things to do. No one in his troupe had any Italian but an officer came to tell them the locals were against Mussolini. This British officer was very friendly, and he was going to be their guide. The captain sat in the front lorry with the sergeant major and the best driver; he was the only one who knew where they were going. They were obviously going deep into Southern Italy and the roads were very narrow and often not more than dirt tracks. Tom was glad he was not driving the lead lorry. The convoy was fairly slow moving so Tom could see a bit of the countryside. Their first stop was a small village where he met some American soldiers.

Tom did not smoke or drink and normally refused his allowance until he came across these Americans who would trade chocolate and chewing gum for beer and particularly cigarettes. Tom liked chewing gum; it kept him concentrating while he was driving. He put this in one of his letters to Marilyn and wondered if the censors would delete it. Marilyn did get several letters full of blanked out portions but chewing gum got through. The only important thing for her was 'love Tom'.

Tom saw very little of Italy except when they stopped at villages for an overnight stay. The rest of the squad was searching out local wines or other pleasures. Tom was enjoying giving cigarettes to the locals, who were very appreciative. Tom had tried wine and thought dilute vinegar better. No one except the captain had any idea where they were or where they were going. The whole troop was in agreement that so far, they were not near the front, and they wanted it to stay that way. Tom talked to the captain and found that before the war he had gone to school in Italy, where his father was working for a motor car company.

After a couple more stops, they could hear gunfire, now the squad became nervous. The captain assured them they would be well back from the front line, and they were here to deliver provisions. He also told them that on the return journey they might have to carry some injured soldiers as they retreated from the front. Now Tom had new people to give his spare cigarettes and share his chewing gum. There were only a few injured soldiers, and their injuries were not life threatening and they all enjoyed a smoke. These fellows were glad to get into the unloaded lorries and go well away from the front.

The drive back to the port was easier and seemed shorter. The Italians at the port were very friendly and it was rumoured that the Italian army had changed sides. It appeared that news was a bit premature; the

Germans were still fighting. The second trip back to the front-line forces seemed longer and the wounded soldiers on the return journey said the Germans were in retreat. They were all thankful for cigarettes from Tom.

Back in the port they loaded their trucks on to a freighter. They were going north to a new port. The captain would leave them, and they would get a new officer to direct their future journeys. The troop all saluted the captain as he left for another assignment and Tom gave a personal farewell. They all had enjoyed his company. All they could glean was that they were going north of Rome. The weather was turning cold and there were no heaters in the cabins only the heat of the engine. At least they were given thick socks and woollen gloves. The landing went well, and they found their trips from the port were shorter. Finally in April 1945 they learnt that the Germans in Italy had surrendered.

Tom was hoping the war was over, but it carried on almost unabated. Luckily for Tom it was over, his squad with their lorries were shipped back to England. He had seen no action and no bullets fired at him. The closest he came was to hear gunfire in the distance. On the other hand the destruction in England was horrific. All the squad was very unhappy to see bomb sites. Tom had thought he would get leave but no such luck. They were transporting provisions all over the country mainly from the ports to the large cities. Tom could not wait to see Marilyn.

The squad was on the outskirts of London when Tom heard and saw the doodle bugs; they were scary. His squad was told to take cover if the engine stopped but the bombs were heading for the centre of London. Tom felt sorry for the people but was glad to get far away from London. The one site that upset him most was in Coventry. They were passing through Coventry when they had to stop at a set of traffic lights (the sergeant major had to obey the road rules in England). A local pointed out the cathedral, it was a total ruin. Tom was not very religious, but that sight put a knot in his stomach. One driver got out and bowed and they had to wait for him to get back in his cab. That night the only topic of conversation was the cathedral. Tom was disappointed they never went through Birmingham; he was keen to see sights he knew.

Finally the war ended but the squad was in northern Scotland delivering groceries. All except the sergeant major and a corporal were conscripts, the rest could not wait to get to base and be demobbed. None of them had leave since being back in Britain and they were impatient but still in the army. There was great rejoicing when they arrived back in Aldershot and everyone except Tom had too much to drink. Tom's demob suit was a poor fit, but he was glad to be out of uniform. As there was no phone at home he surprised his parents, who had saved his twentieth birthday cake.

There were no bomb sites in his parent's area, but his father told him there were plenty in Ladywood where there were many factories.

As it was weekend, he could not see Marilyn until Monday. Suddenly he felt tired, he had been running on adrenaline and now he had to sleep. He slept for twelve hours straight, and his mother checked on him several times. On the Sunday he took a bus to the centre of Birmingham, he just had to see the destruction.

On Monday he was up bright and early and decided he would have to wait until dinner (lunch) time to see Marilyn; that was going to be a long wait. First, he had to see the manager and make sure he had his job back. The manager was glad to see him as they had lots of half fixed or broken machinery. Actually the manager told Tom it was probably against the law to refuse him his old job.

At lunch time Tom walked into the typing pool to be greeted by Marilyn jumping up and down. One of the typists remarked that Tom was very popular, and Marilyn's joyous welcome was out of character. Marilyn had shown many of his letters to her typist friends and they were all looking forward to the reunion. Tom and Marilyn kissed ignoring the clapping onlookers and then decided to go for a walk. Tom suggested no one follow them, all the girls laughed, as if they would.

Tom asked how Marilyn had spent her eighteenth birthday and found it was like any other day. There was no party and no presents and she was confined to the house. Tom admitted his twentieth birthday had been spent driving to Leeds but some of his mates toasted him when they stopped for the night. There was no cake but plenty of potato chips, beer and of course pop for Tom. He marvelled at how much beer his driver mates could consume and still remain standing.

They both loved each other, and Tom asked Marilyn whether she would marry him. She said yes but asked how? Tom said it would take careful planning and to leave it to him. He had heard they could marry in Gretna Green but there were new restrictions. They could not just show up and get married; they had to register in advance. Gretna was just north of Carlisle and on a regular bus route to Glasgow. One weekend Tom decided to take the trip and stay overnight in Glasgow and come back the next day. He also investigated the registration procedure. He thought that a complete journey by bus would be tiring, and he had to investigate another route. He found they could marry on a Saturday but probably not on a Sunday.

Marilyn was eighteen and so Tom started the process of getting passports for her and himself. He used his home address on both applications. During the war his parent's house had bomb damage and they had moved to another suburb. He asked Marilyn if she would go to Canada, she said yes as she wanted to get as far away from her father as possible. Tom noticed when Marilyn spoke about her father, she gritted her teeth and her expression changed. In Italy while talking to the major he had been told to look at facial expressions. The captain put it that the locals were friendly Italians but if he met an unfriendly Italian it would show on his face, no language needed. Tom was thinking that was an important bit of education the army had given him.

Tom got the forms from the Canadian Consulate in Birmingham; they filled them in on their dinner breaks and submitted them. Marilyn was a worried her father would find out. She was very careful what she said to him. Actually she rarely spoke to her father and even her mother. Occasionally he went to the pub in an evening but even then, she spoke very little to her mother. Her mother was a very quiet person and it seemed that she had become cowed by her husband, she was afraid of him.

They were called for an interview at the consulate. Marilyn asked for the afternoon off and her boss said she would not dock her pay or take it out from her holiday allowance. The consular official was very understanding. They showed their documents and he said there was no problem finding them jobs. He said they could sail on the same liner, but he could only arrange single accommodation. If they married, they could contact the liner's office and preferably the purser to change their accommodation. They thanked him and asked for a ship from Glasgow.

When it was time to sail, they planned their 'escape'. They gave two weeks' notice and would leave on the Friday afternoon. Tom decided on a train to Manchester and then a bus to Carlisle. They would sleep in the Carlisle bus station and catch an early bus to Gretna and then later a bus to Glasgow.

Tom had bought a small suitcase which Marilyn kept under her desk. She would wear extra clothes to work and put them in the case. A spare pair of shoes was also spirited away in her handbag. She did her own washing at home so neither her mother nor father suspected anything. Her bedroom had some decorations and small objects, but she decided to leave them so that her mother would not notice.

When they gave in their notice Marilyn asked that the company keep the first week's wages and she would collect two weeks' wages and holiday money when she was leaving the job. She told her father that there had been some mix up with the wages and would get two weeks' wages next Friday.

"Make sure I get my money next Friday."

"Yes Dad."

Marilyn was angry but she tried not to say any more. Her mother had watched on in silence.

As they were leaving on the Friday there was a small celebration and Tom promised to send an update when they were settled. As they boarded the train to Manchester Marilyn was shaking. The train departed before she would normally reach home, so Tom told her not to worry. Tom took her in his arms and told her not to worry she had escaped. Marilyn calmed down on the train and enjoyed the view. She had been nowhere since she was very young and never on a train. The bus ride to Carlisle was long as they stopped at many small towns, but she enjoyed that too. She had two pay packets in her purse and extra holiday money; she felt rich. Tom had worked a lot of overtime and also had money he had saved while in the army. He explained they could find a bed and breakfast in Carlisle, but he wanted to save money. They would try to sleep in the bus station and catch the first bus to Gretna.

They had an uncomfortable night in the bus station and caught the first bus to Gretna. As they were early, they sat on a park bench for a couple of hours. Marilyn was still a bit worried, but Tom was reassuring. The wedding ceremony was simple, and a witness was provided for a few shillings.

Tom was so happy to get the marriage certificate in his hands and told Marilyn her father could do nothing. They caught the bus to Glasgow and found the shipping office. Luckily the purser was in the office. Tom asked him if they could get a cabin. The purser looked at the marriage certificate and smiled when he saw the date. He said the liner was not full and he would see what he could do. The cabin would be an internal one and he hoped they were not claustrophobic. They could board Sunday morning but would have to spend this night in Glasgow.

Marilyn said she was hungry, so they found a fish and chip shop and ate their meal on a park bench. Marilyn was in a very happy mood and hugged Tom. Everything was going to plan and now they had to find a bed and breakfast accommodation. Near the docks they found accommodation. That evening they went to a pub and had sandwiches. As neither of them drank they just had a couple of bottles of pop. Now Marilyn became nervous, she had not been naked in front of anyone since she was very young. She had no pyajamas so would have to sleep in her bra, knickers and under slip. There was also the problem of the noise they would make and maybe the landlady would hear. Tom listened to her fears and realized he would have to be patient. They were both tired and a kiss and a cuddle had them prepared for sleep.

The breakfast was a large one with bacon, eggs, sausages and fried bread. Tom was surprised and told the landlady that it was the biggest breakfast he had had for years. She winked and said it helped to live near the port. She wished them well in their newly married life; she had also seen the marriage certificate.

Tom thought they were too early to board but there was already a queue to board the liner. When they reached the officer taking names Tom gave their maiden names followed by Marilyn's married name.

"Ah special guests, congratulations and welcome, this sailor will take you to your cabin."

Obviously, he had been alerted by the purser. The sailor took them into what seemed to be the bowels of the ship. Tom had been on a ship before, but this was a first time for Marilyn. The cabin was small with two bunk beds a wash basin and a wardrobe for clothes. The sailor said if they shut the door and switched off the light it would be pitch black but there was a night light by the sink. He demonstrated by switching off the light and then switching on the night light. Marilyn gave out a little cry and said she wanted that experience again. Tom had always travelled in cabins with portholes and that was a new experience for him. The sailor gave them a card with mealtimes and their table number and left.

Marilyn stood by the sink with her hand close to the night light switch and asked Tom to switch off the light. She was amazed she could see nothing even the hand in front of her face. Unfortunately, she used the wrong hand and had to search for the switch. Tom had his hand on the light switch but let her fumble about. They both started to laugh; this was their first real laugh for a couple of days, it had broken the tension. They unpacked their meagre clothing, and it was lost in the wardrobe. They proceeded to the dining room and found there was no formal seating for lunch (they would have to learn not to call it dinner). Marilyn and Tom lined up to be served by the crew. They were both amazed at the food on offer. Marilyn took too much food and confessed her eyes were bigger than her belly. Marilyn was fairly skinny, and Tom told her she could put on weight and he would not mind.

After lunch they stood on the deck and watched the ship leave the port. They stood motionless for quite some time with Tom's arm around her shoulder. Marilyn said she felt safe and at ease in his arms and she was watching their new life beginning. As they left the dock, they started to feel the swell and as they left the Firth of Clyde the ship was moving up and down and from side to side. At first it was fun but trying to move with the ship became exhausting. They went to their cabin and lay on their beds. Tom took the top bunk which entailed climbing a ladder. There was also a rail on the side of the bed to stop him falling out. Marilyn also found she had a rail, probably useful in rough weather.

At dinner they went to their table and found they were seated with three middle-aged couples. As they were sitting down one lady asked when they were married. Tom told them yesterday and everyone laughed including Marilyn. That broke the ice and then everyone was talking. Marilyn looked at the menu and saw most of the items she did not know and had never eaten. Fried calf's brains, kippers, smoked salmon and roast buffalo stuck in her brain, and she determined to try all of them. Tonight she only wanted a light meal as the rocking motion might not be good for her stomach later.

After the meal Marilyn admitted to Tom that she enjoyed talking with her mouth half full. At home, meals were in silence and if she wanted to cough, she had to leave the table. If she wanted to sneeze, she had to leave the room. Tom was wondering at this; in his squad no one left the table even to fart. Of course he did not tell Marilyn about these 'unusual' habits. He was thinking that he had to give her time to experience the way of the world. She had led a very sheltered life.

They decided that it was too rough to sleep together so they separated after a long kiss. The night started a bit rough and then they both fell asleep. Tom awoke early in the morning and the ship was not rocking. Marilyn had made him leave the main light on overnight and so he easily found the door to go down the hall to have a pee. When he returned Marilyn was awake and wanted to do the same. She was amazed that she told Tom what she wanted. This freedom was so new to her. She was laughing to herself as she sat on the lavatory, she was feeling so free.

Breakfast was a revelation. Marilyn had the fried calf's brains and loved them. The kippers were too difficult to eat as she was trying to sort through the bones. Pancakes with maple syrup were her favourite. Everyone else including Tom seemed to stick to the normal English breakfast. Marilyn was pleased with herself she was being adventurous. Tom found that only one couple were immigrants the other two were visiting relatives. The next surprise for their new friends were that Tom and Marilyn did not drink. There was wine even at breakfast. Tom told them of his time in Italy and that he preferred dilute vinegar to wine. That had everyone laughing and even Marilyn was asking whether she should try wine. The advice from the table was that she should try a sweet wine.

On deck the breeze was quite cold, and they retired to a sitting room. Marilyn was fascinated by the dresses the women were wearing. She had very few clothes and their wardrobe easily accommodated what they had in two small suitcases. When they went out on deck Marilyn was shivering and a lady came up and gave her a jacket. Marilyn asked how she could return it and the lady told it was hers. Marilyn and Tom were speechless. Apparently, word of their new marriage had spread amongst the other passengers. Like any small village, news travelled very fast.

That coat came in useful as they neared Canada; they saw small icebergs. These were only just sticking out above water, but they were reminded that there was a lot of ice underwater. The captain assured the passengers they would steer clear of any icebergs. Tom was thinking he was a very poor swimmer and had no idea whether Marilyn could swim. Marilyn was enjoying mealtimes she was trying everything. She loved smoked salmon, and it was better than cooked salmon. She tried buffalo steak as she assumed she would never eat it again; little did she know. Escargot was a dish she loved and asked for more even though she was told about the dish. The waiter said very few English passengers would eat the dish and apologized that they had no frogs' legs. He told her she could get them in Quebec. Tom was amazed at what his wife was eating; his tastes were much more conservative.

After lunch on the second day they retired to their cabin and Marilyn stripped to her knickers and bra. Tom was taken aback and quickly stripped off and put on a condom. In the army they were issued with plenty of condoms as getting a venereal disease was a punishable offence. He had never used one but had been instructed as how the put one on. Marilyn lay on her bed and invited him to join her. The bed was small and cramped and so he climbed on top of her. Entering was a bit difficult and Marilyn had to smother a laugh but when it happened, she took a deep breath. Tom was doing all the work, but Marilyn was enjoying every minute she was not sure what to expect. Tom climaxed but had nowhere to go so he just lay on top of Marilyn. She did not mind she just loved to be close to Tom.

Later Tom asked her why she had decided on the afternoon. Marilyn said it prepared her for dinner and did not spoil breakfast. Tom was marvelling at his new wife she was so honest. He reminded her they were both virgins and her reply were that they could only get better.

They were both looking forward to getting off the ship although they were having a great time. Sailing down the St. Lawrence was magical; they were seeing sights they had never dreamed of. Marilyn was saying she wanted to get off and explore. They docked at Quebec City only this was lower Quebec City. They cleared customs and immigration and there was a bus to take them to the centre of Quebec City. They were both blown away with this city.

Tom asked if she had any French and she had taken a little at school but could remember nothing. Tom had a little French and some Italian. They went to a café and Tom tried a bit of French and then a little Italian. The waitress was laughing and asked them to speak English. Marilyn asked whether they had frogs' legs, and the waitress could not stop laughing. She told Marilyn they would have to go to a good restaurant, but she recommended the dish. She admitted no English person had ever asked for that dish.

When they returned to the ship Marilyn was saying she must learn French. Tom was amazed that his wife was enjoying everything better than him, except sex. Next stop Montreal where they would all disembark. All their table mates were wishing them the best of luck in their new life. Tom was thanking them all for a pleasant voyage and watching his liberated wife. Marilyn looked around their cabin and thanked the cabin that a small space had made her so excited, and it would live in her memory. Tom was listening and shaking his head. He admitted to himself that the cabin was a special place that would last in his memory.

At Montreal dock they were met and taken to the train station and saw little of the city. Next stop Toronto where they were put on a train to Hamilton. It was all so efficient but there was no time to see anything. Marilyn was always poking Tom to see some new sight. In Hamilton they were taken to a boarding house where the madam owner was pleased that they only needed one room. She could let the other one. The landlady said the other residents were men and they should be quiet. Marilyn told her they were quiet lovemakers. Tom was standing there open-mouthed; he was wondering at this free spirit he had unleashed.

The next day they were introduced to their new work. The factories were next to each other and within walking distance. Tom was introduced to a lot of poorly maintained machinery and Marilyn entered a typing pool where no one had shorthand. They both fit in very well and could get as much overtime as they wanted. Both their managers were pleased to meet them. Tom was keen to get a place 'of their own'. Marilyn was uncomfortable with the way some of the borders were looking at her. Within a few weeks they found a furnished flat and moved to more comfortable surroundings.

They were warned that summer could be hot and humid, but fall was the best time of year. Tom's boss was very pleased with him and took them out to a barbecue during one of the weekends. This was the time when they mingled with Canadians. Marilyn loved barbecued meat whatever variety, Tom also loved the food and the company. He told some stories about his war, and he was very popular. It turned out that there was an Italian family at the barbecue, and they latched on to Tom. Tom and Marilyn were invited to their house the following weekend.

Tom and Marilyn arrived at a party in full swing. There was plenty of food and drink and they were all surprised when Tom said they did not drink. The host had arranged a taxi to take them home. Marilyn told them she liked exotic food. One of the ladies brought out the stinkiest ripe cheese she could find. Marilyn put it on a biscuit and ate it. The men were rolling around in laughter and challenging their women to do the same. Tom entertained them with stories of Southern Italy. As they left the host was telling them to come to his house anytime. Several of the guests were inviting them to visit they wanted to hear more about Southern Italy.

Life in Hamilton settled into a good routine. Tom asked if he should send a letter to one of Marilyn's friends in the office. At first, she was hesitant and then realized her father could never find her. Tom had arranged a post box and that gave Marilyn more confidence. That started a transatlantic correspondence. The typing pool was being acquainted with life in Canada.

Winter was not too bad in Hamilton and Tom and Marilyn were earning plenty of money with lots of overtime. Tom was contemplating buying a place of their own when his manager came up with a suggestion.

"Tom you are too good for this place you could earn much more up north. I have a friend who will visit in a few weeks. He owns a car yard and an engineering workshop. He wants someone to run the engineering workshop. Talk to him I think this is an opportunity, but Northern Ontario is a difficult place to live."

Tom discussed it with Marilyn, and she was excited and asked if she could meet this fellow. They were having great sex and Tom realized Marilyn was the driving force in this marriage. Tom did not know where they might go but Marilyn did not care. They met Dimitry in a restaurant and Marilyn was first to ask questions. He explained that his father was Ukrainian and came to Canada after WW1. He had come to work in the mines but his skill as a mechanic led him into fixing vehicles and machinery. He opened a car and lorry workshop and then a workshop to make and fix things used in the mining industry. At this point he asked if they would like a drink. When they both asked for soft drinks he sat back in his chair, laughed and said if they came to North Bay, they would be unique. He did not know anyone who did not drink and that included the Native Canadians.

Dimitry wanted to concentrate on his car business, his father had just died and now he was trying to run both businesses. Marilyn interrupted and asked if she could have a job. Dimitry's reply was that she could be company secretary and he was enjoying negotiating with a woman. Tom was sitting back watching his wife take over. Then Marilyn shocked them both when she asked if they could buy the engineering business. There was silence for a couple of minutes.

"I have never met such a couple and I think I need a few drinks before I can answer that question."

"I am sure your father would not like his engineering works to fail but we will make it succeed."

"You have now crossed several boundaries and if you were a man, I might start swearing but my father is telling me to give in."

"Now we have to discuss money."

"You are cruel, but I am glad my competitors don't employ you."

Tom was sitting quietly watching and marvelling at Marilyn. She had sewn up a good deal and all he had to do was agree. They both had to resign their positions and asked about how to get to North Bay. Dimitry said that the drive to North Bay was about three hundred miles and to do it in two days not to try it all at once. They had a second-hand car but Dimitry promised them a car more suitable for Northern

Ontario when they arrived. Both Marilyn's boss and Tom's boss were unhappy to see them go but both said they would succeed.

The drive to North Bay was long and they stopped overnight on the way. This was spring and Marilyn loved the scenery she was definitely going to learn to drive. Some of the roads were not more than dirt tracks and Tom was wondering whether his car would make the journey. Finally they drove into Dimitry's car yard to be greeted by at least twenty people. Dimitry introduced his mother who was a local Indian and very glad to meet a woman who had beaten her son. Marilyn hugged and kissed her, Tom and Dimitry stood back and watched these women make a memorable contact. Dimity's wife was from Yorkshire and Tom immediately made a connection as one of the army drivers was from Yorkshire.

Dimitry showed them the car workshop and the engineering workshop down the road. He took Tom's car and promised a better car the next day. Then he showed them their flat on the second floor of a four-storey building. Marilyn could not believe their luck, but Dimitry's mother said they needed more furniture. The next day they were awoken with new furniture.

Now they set about getting the engineering workshop in shape. Marilyn was going through all the books and also working for the car dealership. Dimitry said his mother, whose name was Kayla, wanted to adopt Marilyn, she would like to have a daughter rather than a son. His mother had a dry sense of humour.

Dimitry explained that hunting was big in the spring, summer and fall and ice hockey and ice fishing popular in winter. The summer would be hot, and the mosquitoes could be large and vicious. His mother made an insect repellent out of some plants, and she would not tell him the recipe.

"My mom is a full-blown member of the Nipissing tribe and as such she has lots of hunting and fishing rights. I am half so I have less rights, you will need a hunting and fishing license. They are easy to get and cheap, have you ever hunted?"

"No, I fired a rifle in the army but never had chance to hunt, what do you hunt?"

"We hunt mainly deer for the venison, occasionally buffalo and rarely moose. We kill wolves if we get a chance. I will take you hunting one day when you get your licenses. I suggest you buy boots and some warm clothes for the winter; it can get very cold here."

The first winter was so cold Tom was wondering whether they could take another. Before winter set in they went hunting and Tom bagged a deer. They dragged it back to the truck and showed Marilyn on their return. She was upset that they had left her in the office and not taken her hunting. One of Kayla's relative skinned and divided the carcass taking bits that Europeans would not eat. Dimitry explained that a kill at the beginning of winter could be stored outside but the kill during fall had to be eaten quickly as they had no large freezer facilities.

Marilyn wanted to kill a buffalo; she had eaten it on the ship and wanted to try it again. Dimitry told her it would have to be a hunting party as once killed they would have to drag it to a suitable vehicle. Buffalos were large beasts and had to be killed not just wounded. The first problem was to find the herd.

Marilyn went on the hunt but was getting tired trudging through fresh snow. One of the Native Canadians killed a buffalo and then there was the task of dragging it back to their vehicle. Marilyn watched the fascinating procedure with several ropes being pulled by several men. The carcass was carved up and Marilyn got a large piece of the fillet, now she had to find out how to cook it. Kayla came to the rescue and carved it for her. Part was cooked in a casserole and part barbecued. Marilyn and Kayla had become good friends.

Ice fishing was good except Dimitry had to set up the tent and drill the hole in the ice. All Tom had to do was run from the car and drop a line through the hole and wait. His first fish was a surprise. Tom tossed it outside the tent onto the ice where it froze. While fishing they had time to chat.

"My mother is quite a character, my father used to tell me to listen to my mother when she talks seriously. The only problem is that I don't know when she is not serious. She is the one who told me to go to Hamilton to find something new. When I came back and told her about Marilyn, she was very anxious to see her. When they met, she said although Marilyn was a different tribe there seemed to be a spiritual connection. She likes my wife but loves Marilyn."

"Marilyn said something similar, she said Kayla was like a new mother."

They caught several fish, and it was so cold Dimitry decided to leave the hut, others could use it. Again Kayla showed Marilyn how to fillet and cook the fish.

Tom was fixing machinery and teaching new employees how to use the machinery. Marilyn was both secretary and saleswoman for the engineering factory and the car dealership. Dimitry was very pleased she had taken a big load off him. Kayla was jokingly telling him to give up and let Marilyn take over. This time Dimitry could not tell whether his mom was joking.

Tom was getting used to the cold temperatures. He started to prefer Centigrade to Fahrenheit, it made more sense to him. -25 centigrade was simpler than trying to convert to Fahrenheit or vice versa. Several days were -25 centigrade and at night it could get colder. Dimitry had warned him that continual very cold temperatures could have an effect on the way you think. Tom was a bit sceptical until one night. He had worked late and drove into the garage. He was so impatient to get into the apartment he forgot to plug the car into the heater. In the garage there was a plug and dangling from the bonnet of the car was a socket. This kept the engine warm during the night or day. In the morning, the car would not start, and Tom went outside to see if he could get a taxi. Five minutes out in the cold had him rushing indoors. He then started to shake, the fifty-degree change in temperature had his body reacting to the change.

Dimitry always had a car to pick up his employees which included Marilyn. Tom had a ride to work and learned a good lesson. As winter turned to spring daytime temperatures were about zero and the ice on the lake was retreating. Marilyn was planning a short vacation; Kayla had taken her into Quebec, and she was picking up a bit of Quebecois and now she wanted to visit a big town. They decided to drive to Hull (pronounced Ull) which was opposite Ottawa. Marilyn found a restaurant with frogs' legs and Tom watched her consume them with relish, his filet mignon was very good. Marilyn loved Hull and she could use some of her Quebecoise.

The next year passed very well. They now owned half of the engineering company and Dimitry was happy as his car business was expanding. Kayla was inviting Marilyn to all sorts of indigenous gatherings and Marilyn was inducted into the tribe. Tom was watching his wife take over. He was just happy to boss his warehouse. As summer approached Marilyn suggested they take a holiday and go to England. Tom was all for it.

Tom planned their journey. They would drive to Montreal and park their car on a lot owned by one of Dimitry's friends. Flying from Montreal was possible to London or Manchester. Marilyn chose Manchester it was her first taste of freedom. They would catch a bus to Birmingham and stay with Tom's parents. In the coming days they would visit the factory and then go to Marilyn's parent's house.

On the flight from Toronto Tom was snoozing but Marilyn was wide awake. She was looking at her passport with the photo of a young girl, now she was a woman. She was remembering their escape from her father. She was shaking in her shoes until the ship left the dock. She had suddenly felt liberated. The memory of the first time and that small cabin had her smiling, pitch black was a special experience. It was the first time she had felt really happy. The lady who gave her the coat showed there were other good people in the world besides Tom. Canada had given her so many chances to show how she could succeed and now she was going to visit old friends in the office. She was feeling confident and self-assured.

Arriving at Manchester airport she felt on top of the world. She decided that on their next visit they would come by sea. The bus to Birmingham was OKAY but next time they would take the train. They both enjoyed the taxi to Tom's parents' place. Tom's parents were very welcoming and loved having them and listening to fantastic stories. Not much had changed in the district except Tom thought the coffee had improved and there seemed a lot more litter.

The visit to the factory was a success, Marilyn was a star in the typing pool. The girls were all impressed with how Marilyn was dressed. Marilyn had a grey suit that was well designed; she had picked it up in Montreal. In Montreal she had to use English and French but not Parisian French but Quebecoise. When she told them her best friend was a Native Canadian and Marilyn was part of the tribe, the girls were all aghast. The girls were all interested in Marilyn's bangle. It had been given her by Kayla so she would have a safe journey. She told them lots of stories and the one about the buffalo was very popular. Frogs' legs had most of them cringing and escargot had their eyes rolling. Tom was able to get a few words in, but Marilyn was dominating the proceedings.

One of her friends said to Tom that the change in Marilyn was remarkable; she was such a quiet girl. What happened?

"Freedom from her father, marriage and the environment in Canada all contributed. As soon as she got married it was as though chains were lifted from her. She now lives life to the full. Marilyn is a driving force in the company and the owner cannot but be happy with the way she is making the company grow."

"Maybe I should go to Canada."

"Go with an open mind and get over home sickness quickly and if you are willing to learn and adapt you will prosper. I think it is best if you have a husband to help you."

"Tom you may be reading my mind."

After leaving the office Tom knew they had to visit Marilyn's parents, but he was not too happy. There had been no communication with her parents and their visit would be a surprise, but it was their duty. Marilyn bought a bottle of wine to celebrate their wedding. Marilyn loved the thought that their wedding was different, and she was going to tell her parents about their flight, she was assuming they would be welcome. They knocked on the door and when her father saw Tom, he rushed at him and grabbed him by the throat. Marilyn cried merde (shit). Marilyn had the bottle in her hand and used it to bash her father's head. He released his grip and sank to the ground. Luckily, the bottle did not break. Her mother stood with an open mouth, she did not move or say anything.

Marilyn stood over her father and said, "No one throttles my husband; particularly not my father! Let's go; if he wakes up, I may have to hit him again."

Yellowknife, very far from Birmingham

Sheila told the immigration officer she did not care whether it was, hot or cold she would go anywhere. She was thinking she had been a bit rash, but she really wanted to get away from Birmingham and anywhere in Canada was okay with her. The immigration officer was delighted he could fill a position he thought he could never fill. Sheila had just broken up with her long-time boyfriend and wanted to go anywhere as long it was far from him. The immigration officer understood she wanted to go far away from England, and he was sending her to a part of Canada that was about as far as you could go. Sheila was heading for Yellowknife in the Yukon to work for a mining company. The immigration officer was wondering whether he had made a mistake. Time would tell he made the correct decision.

Leonid was the manager of the mining company in Yellowknife. He had come to Canada as a refugee and because he had lived in the Arctic and knew about mining, he was sent to Yellowknife. Leonid had two sisters, one younger and one older. His sister was born in 1938, he was born in 1939 and his younger sister in 1940. They were all born in Moscow and as his father was a military officer, they were transferred to Riga. For the Soviet Union, the war started in 1941. Leonid's father, his mother and sisters had to escape Riga to get to Moscow. The train they were on was strafed by German aircraft. Their father was able to get them under the train carriage. With three children this was a harrowing experience for Leonid's mother, but she relied on her husband to keep them safe.

As their father was an army officer the family was given an apartment in Moscow. He was then transferred to a battalion that was to operate behind enemy lines. Unfortunately, they were spotted by a German reconnaissance plane and surrounded by German forces. The General in charge surrendered and the officers were sent to Buchenwald. The general committed suicide as he knew Stalin would have him executed. Leonid's mother had no idea whether her husband was dead or alive. She could keep the flat while there was uncertainty but that was only temporary.

At the end of the war the prisoners were released from Buchenwald and Stalin had the officers sent to the Arctic Circle to the coal mines in Vorkuta. This was a gulag for criminals and political prisoners. Leonid's father had a secret he wished to keep. He was previously an officer of the NKVD (precursor to the KGB). Many of the miners would have loved to kill him if they had known. As he was an engineer the management put him in charge of machine maintenance. The mine had a quota system to fill and broken-down machinery was always a problem. He was supposed to keep all machinery running. This was a gigantic problem with -30 centigrade temperatures and inevitable breakdowns.

Stalin died in 1953 and in 1955 Leonid and his younger sister, Mila were allowed to visit their father. After a three-day train journey, they reached Vorkuta; since they had little food, they were hungry. Luckily, a lady on the train gave them some *pilmeni* and *kvass* (dumplings and a drink made from rye bread and yeast). Their father was happy to see them but could offer them little comfort. He did have a little money for the return journey. He took them in the cage down to the mine and Leonid was disturbed by the way the miners looked at his sister. Their father agreed this was not the place for a fifteen-year-old girl. Within three days they left for Moscow, both father and son breathed a sigh of relief.

Their father was released in 1958 and went to his parents in Belarus. Leonid decided he would go to live with his father at least for a while. The problem was that there was no room in his grandparent's house; he had to live with his aunt. His aunt was very strict, no alcohol, no swearing and regular attendance at church. Leonid's other problem was that he could be drafted into the army. He consulted his father who advised he escape to the West. He should go to Poland and not Germany as the Soviets controlled Germany; he should not try to cross the border in a big city but try in a country area.

Leonid did cross the border and was sent to a refugee camp. The Poles were thinking of sending him back to Russia, but the Red Cross intervened. He told them he had been in the coal mine in Vorkuta and enjoyed the far north. He did not tell them he had only spent three days in Vorkuta. The Canadians were interested in mining experience in the Arctic Circle. Leonid had said the correct things and was off to Canada; he had no idea about Canada but at least he was not being sent back to Russia. In the camp he had no chance to consult maps but when he did, he was astounded at the size of Canada.

In the refugee camp he had learned some English, he was a quick learner. He knew he had to improve his English and this trip to Canada was going to give him the chance. The train took him to Amsterdam, and he crossed borders with no problem. He did not have a passport but a refugee document with his photo and name. The border authorities would just looked at the document and said okay. Leonid was not used to this informality and when they took him to the dock, he looked at the liner; it was the biggest thing he had ever seen. He boarded the liner without anyone asking him a question. His cabin had a porthole and there were three other men sharing this space that seemed bigger than his mother's whole flat. There were two other Russians and one fellow from the Ukraine, they all spoke Russian. Leonid realized he would have to get out of this group to learn more English. Actually it was no problem as this group was all discussing politics and Leonid knew nothing about politics and was not interested to learn. He was free to go on deck night or day.

Besides looking out to sea the real pleasure was the food. Leonid was a growing lad with an appetite to match. One of the Russians complained there was no Russian food. He was shouted down by the rest who said this food was the best they had tasted. Leonid had eaten well at his auntie's but here there was so much choice. There was a menu and that helped Leonid with his reading. On deck he had met an English sailor who helped him with spoken English. The sailor asked where he was going, Leonid told him Yellowknife and hoped it was near the sea. It took a long time before the sailor stopped laughing. He then took Leonid to the library and introduced him to the atlases. Leonid first saw how big Canada was and the position of Yellowknife. The sailor told him he was going to a place in Canada almost as far as you could get from the sea. Now he was introduced to the library he was there every day until they reached the St. Lawrence River.

Except for meals he was on deck all the time. He was looking at farmland and many churches with spires. He thought his aunt would love this place. He did not know the difference between Russian Orthodox and French Catholic. He was fascinated by boats pulling tree trunks all tied together. As they came closer to the shore people were waving and he was waving back. His impression was that this was a friendly country. His cabin mates came on deck to look at their new land. The other three were going to Ontario and when he showed them the map and where he was going, they were all astounded. As they disembarked, they all hugged and hoped that this would be a good new life.

Leonid was on trains for several days, first from Montreal to Toronto. In Toronto he was put up in a hotel and his room had a shower and a bidet. He worked out the bidet was there to wash his bum. He enjoyed the sensation and tried it several times. From Toronto there were lots of flat lands. He was later to learn these were the Prairies. He shared a compartment meant for four with only one passenger a talkative Canadian. That was good for Leonid he could sense the difference in accent with the English sailor. Leonid got off the train at Edmonton and was escorted to a train bound for Yellowknife. By this time he was fed up with trains.

Arriving in Yellowknife in the autumn he was feeling the cold, but the immigration people supplied him with winter clothes. He was to work at a gold mine, and this was nothing like a coal mine. His father had told him that maintaining machinery was important for productivity. Now he told the mine manager in broken English he had experience in maintaining machinery. He had no experience but learned on the job. As his English improved, the management saw potential in this young man. He was good with the workers and always had good ideas.

After two years he was the mine manager. Yellowknife was a place where workers came to make money and would then move on after one winter. Leonid had persuaded the mine owners to set up a workshop where they could fix machinery and make parts. This turned out to be a profitable venture as other companies were coming to fix machinery and order new parts. Leonid started to understand that gold mining was on the decline in Yellowknife, but he enjoyed living in this small city.

The expanding business meant he needed help and he put in an advert for a secretary. He was very surprised when Sheila arrived. She was a typist with shorthand and very good looking. There were not many single good-looking girls in Yellowknife. Leonid thought his payday had come in. Payday was one of those phrases he had picked up from the workers. There were many other phrases and words they had taught him, many not repeatable in good company. He had a typist, but he wanted someone to organize the office and this lady had all the credentials.

Sheila had left Birmingham on a train to Liverpool. She was to take a liner from Liverpool to Toronto. There would then be a long journey across

Canada to Yellowknife in the Yukon. Sheila was now wondering whether she had done the right thing. She wanted to escape but did she have to go so far? The liner was a pleasure as she was seated during dining with middle-aged people. There were a few young men on board, but she had given them all the cold shoulder; she was not interested in men. She loved the St. Lawrence, Quebec, Montreal and Toronto. The immigration officer had noticed she was going to the Yukon.

"It is summer, but the temperature could be anywhere from 15 to 30 centigrade. Sorry I can't translate to Fahrenheit."

"I can" was Sheila's reply.

Now she was on the Canadian Pacific thankfully with a sleeper which she would need. She had been advised she would disembark in Edmonton and then fly to Yellowknife. This would be her first flight and she was nervous.

At Yellowknife Airport she was met by Leonid, a very good-looking young man; he was to be her boss. Sheila had very little luggage, but Leonid carried it to the car. Yellowknife was a small town, but Sheila did notice what she though was a lake and very few people on the street. Leonid took her to a small apartment where she would live. She called it a flat, a new word for Leonid. They deposited her luggage and then drove to the office. The mine was on the edge of town. Leonid explained her duties then started to tell her about the night life. There were a few bars which he did not recommend, a picture house and a dance hall.

"I came here for two years to earn some money, but I am not interested in romance."

Leonid was shocked but told her it was okay. After she had said that about romance, she started to think that maybe he was married.

"Is there a library I like to read?"
"Yes, we all stock up on books before winter comes."

Actually he found long periods of reading difficult except when it was science or engineering. They drove to the library where she could register and get some books. The librarian was glad to get a new customer and showed her around the library. Leonid told her there was a radio in the 'flat' and a car would pick her up the next day at nine a.m. She also saw the bank, which was close to the library; she was very interested in the bank.

The next day an older man chauffeured her to work, he was not very talkative which was okay with Sheila. In the office she met Rhonda who was an older lady employed as a part-time typist. Entering Leonid's office Sheila asked, "do you mind if I call you Len your name does not role off my tongue?"

This phrase was new to Leonid, but he remembered it for future use.

"No in fact I like Len and I think I will use it. Now this office is a mess do you think you can put it in order, poor Rhonda can hardly keep up with the typing. Also English is my second language and I often need help."

"I like a challenge and I suggest you tell me what you want to say in letters or reports, and I will use my shorthand. I will correct any English mistakes and if you agree we will get on well."

"That sounds ideal to me. I want to expand this business as gold mining is probably going to go in decline."

Sheila thought she had been hard on him, but she had to get their working relation in order. She soon had the office in shape and organized a new filing system. Rhonda was very friendly, and Sheila helped her with her typing. Sheila was invited to Rhonda's house for dinner and found her husband was the chauffer. They were long term residents and her husband had been injured in the mine and now worked in the workshop. He explained that he was afraid to get friendly with a pretty young lady as his wife would beat him. They all had a good laugh, and it was a good start to the evening. This dinner gave her a lot of local information she could not get from frequent visits to the library.

Sheila avoided visiting any of the local bars and the dance hall. The picture house seemed to have a lot of old films, but she liked many of them. It seemed that new films took a long time to get to Yellowknife. Going out in the evening in summer was no problem as it was light until about 11pm. Yellowknife was about

400km south of the Arctic Circle and one attraction was the northern lights. Sheila loved the lights it gave her a feeling of being alone and happy. As autumn approached daylight seemed to reduce rapidly and she started to see foxes and even a coyote. She did not recognize that animal and had to ask her driver. Ralph, the driver, told her it was a coyote and there were grizzly bears in the region, but they did not come into town. Now she became interested in the wildlife in the Yukon. Asking questions in the library introduced her to a more intimate friendship with the librarian, an older woman. As the nights drew in, she was going to the library less as it was getting dark and cold after work. She only started visiting the library at weekends where she met an older man who was half Native Canadian. He was on one of the local Native Canadian councils and he wanted to know about other places in the world. He was particularly interested how English people hunted and fished. Sheila explained that there was very little hunting except for the rich. They hunted deer and pheasant on closed estates. Fishing in the rivers was popular with the ordinary people but the fish were not often large enough to eat. This amused her new friend. The evening's entertainment was mainly reading or listening to the radio and of course cooking.

Len asked her whether she could drive, and her answer was in the negative. He suggested if she learned to drive the company could let her have a car.

She talked to Rhonda who said her husband Ralph would teach her to drive. She obtained a Provisional License and soon passed her test. Len was seeing this girl was a fast learner. He took her to a meeting with one of the owners and she took the meeting down in shorthand. At this first meeting she kept quiet but vowed if she went to another meeting, she would have some impact.

While they were driving Ralph told her lots of stories and gave some advice. He told her to buy some snowshoes as when snow started to fall it could be around for at least four months. Wear two pairs of gloves, an inner pair not too thick and an outer pair of thick material, particularly skin. Long Johns were a must and thermal underwear was also required. Sheila smiled, here was a man talking about her underwear. Ralph asked her whether she had ever been hunting. Her reply was that she had never held a gun. Ralph and Rhonda would take her into the woods so she could have practice. Ralph said that just before winter set in they would go hunting and try to bag a deer. He would take along a local Native Canadian friend because if he wounded a deer, they would have to track it till it was finally dead. Due to his disability his friend would do the tracking.

Sheila was quietly excited about going hunting. Her friend in the library had talked about hunting but she never believed she would hunt. One Sunday

Sheila, Rhonda and Ralph went into the woods and Ralph handed her a rifle.

"What do I shoot?"

"You will shoot nothing live until you have mastered this rifle. I see you are left-handed so put the butt into your left shoulder and steady the gun with your right hand and pull the trigger with your left index finger. In winter you will remove the outer glove and never pull the trigger, with bare fingers your skin will stick to the trigger. Always point a loaded gun away from yourself and your companions, generally towards the ground well in front of your feet. Our hospital gets several casualties each year where men have shot themselves in the foot, so far, I don't think a woman has done that. After a few shots Ralph said that was enough, Sheila was disappointed, but he told her she could have a sore shoulder on Monday. Sure enough she awoke on Monday with a sore shoulder. She had felt the force of the butt on her shoulder but thought it was not painful. Rhonda explained she was being hit in a place that was not used to punishment. She was told she would be all right in a couple of days and next time her shoulder would be less painful.

The following Sunday Ralph set up some targets at various heights. Sheila was hitting these stationary targets regularly. Ralph told her the chances of hitting a stationary deer were slim, now she had to focus on a target to the left of the main target and then move to the right and shoot the target. After a few shots Sheila had mastered the art and was a good shot. Ralph called a halt and Sheila said this was the most fun she had had since coming to Yellowknife.

Len started to see a very happy young secretary and she told him about Ralph's shooting tuition. She wanted to go on a hunt as soon as possible, she was dreaming about shooting a deer.

"Actually, Ralph taught me to shoot, and I have been hunting with him several times. He is a very patient man and to go hunting with him is a pleasure. He has lots of Native Canadian friends and they are very useful when you have to drag a carcass to a vehicle. They skin and butcher the animals and take parts that Europeans don't eat."

Sheila had thought about killing an animal but not what happened after that. Dragging a dead carcass and skinning the animal sent a shiver down her spine.

Len explained that when winter set in he would have to take the car as she had no garage. He showed her the garage at the office where there was an electrical socket in each bay. This was used with a plug hanging from each vehicle to keep the engine warm. She had been driving the car for weeks but had not noticed the plug. Len said she would always have transport and not to try walking any distance in the cold weather. Sheila could not wait for winter to come. Rhonda cautioned her that in winter people did strange things. The prolonged cold and very little daylight had a negative effect on some people. They felt trapped indoors and many marriages did not survive winter. This was a very young community, and Ralph and Rhonda were older than most of the population. They had come to Yellowknife many years ago and fell in with the lifestyle. They made friends with the local Native Canadians and that was one of the reasons that kept them in Yellowknife.

The first snow fell, and Sheila had a chance try her snowshoes. Ralph explained they were most useful in deep fine snow. She was to find out how useful they were on her first hunt. Ralph's local friend found a small herd and then Ralph judged the wind. They had to be down wind and move very slowly. Ralph said she should pick an animal, take aim and fire. Now Sheila was very nervous, so Ralph told her to take a deep breath and relax. Her first shot missed the deer but Ralph had anticipated the deer's movement and hit it with his shot. Unfortunately, he did not kill it and then the chase began. Ralph and Sheila soon tired and the Native Canadian tracked the animal and killed it.

This was a large male and Sheila helped drag the animal to a place where the truck could drive. Suddenly she looked at this dead deer and tears welled up and she had to wipe them away.

"We did not kill this animal for sport, it will keep us in meat for part of the winter. The Native Canadians will enjoy their portion and some lesser male in the herd will have more fun."

That amused Sheila and she started to laugh. The Native Canadians wondered why she was laughing and when Ralph explained they were all laughing. Sheila asked Ralph what she did wrong, she missed.

"This is your first hunt; you were excited, and your aim suffered. We have many hunts where we do not shoot any animals. It may take many hunts before you kill a beast."

"What beasts do you shoot?"

"We only hunt deer; if we see a wolf, we will shoot it. If a grizzly attacks we will shoot it, but most times they move away from us. Generally they will smell us from a distance. We do not shoot foxes nor coyotes, nor birds and we try not to shoot other humans. We have to take time to identify our prey. The other men will butcher the deer and I will get a few pieces of the best meat. As you were the first to shoot you will get the best piece of fillet. I have a large freezer and we can store the meat there. Rhonda will show you how to cook the meat. This is wild venison and can be tough."

That night Sheila found she was very tired and had a good sleep. She was dreaming of lying in the snow aiming her rifle, but it would not fire. At the office, Rhonda was waiting with congratulations. Sheila said she missed but Ralph said it was a near miss. Rhonda said she had been on several hunts before she hit a deer. Len said he would come on the next hunt. Ralph had shown him how to shoot and now he wanted to watch Sheila shoot.

Sheila could not wait for the next Sunday. It was getting very cold, and the snow was deeper. Ralph had told everyone that Sheila would have the first shot and Len and he would pick the sides they thought the deer would run. This time Sheila calmed herself down by thinking of the library and the need to keep quiet. Her shot hit the deer and Len's shot downed the animal. The locals moved in and made sure it was dead. They were happy they had no trekking to do. They all retired to the waiting vehicles and Len pulled out a bottle of Vodka. Ralph told him, "Later. Not in front of the locals." Ralph explained he never drank in front of any Native Canadians, even those who were his friends. The Native Canadians had no tolerance for alcohol, and this was the biggest problem the elders of the tribe were fighting. He knew all the elders and listened to their stories.

At Ralph's place they toasted their kill. Sheila had not tasted alcohol since coming to Canada. She tried one small glass of vodka but decided that it was too strong for her. Ralph said she should try one of his home brewed wines. He recommended Lemon and Potato and Sheila loved it. He gave her a bottle to take home and cautioned that it was a live wine and she should keep it in the fridge and loosen the cork occasionally to relieve the pressure.

Sheila was now starting to enjoy living in Yellowknife, but winter was settling in and daylight was diminishing. She thought that it would not be a problem, but she seemed more depressed. She enjoyed visiting Rhonda and Ralph but on other days when she was not working, she was bored. Len sensed she was not her happy self, so he organized an ice-fishing competition with some of the workers. He invited Ralph and Sheila to his tent on the ice. Each group of three would have a tent and at ten a.m. would drill a hole in the ice and at midday they would stop fishing and the biggest catch would get a prize. Sheila thought this would not be interesting but after the hole was drilled, they all put a line into the lake and held on to their line.

Sheila was first to get a bite and she pulled up a large fish. Ralph took it off the hook and threw it out onto the ice. Now Sheila was excited and released her line into the hole as quick as she could. Len pulled out vodka and they toasted the first catch. Sheila had a sip but was too intent on her line. After catching three fish she was drinking a whole glass. Len put the bottle away as he did not want to get her drunk. They did not win but Sheila said they should do this again; now she was not feeling the cold. Ralph and Len took her home and she was soon asleep.

Every morning Ralph told her the temperature and when it reached -30C she translated it to Fahrenheit. Ralph admitted he could not understand Fahrenheit.

Rhonda was advising her on various subjects and Sheila thought she should be a psychologist rather than a typist. In the evening she was bored; Rhonda told her to get jigsaw puzzles from the library. They had many jigsaws and in winter they were very popular.

"I am hopeless at jigsaws."

"That is good because you will not finish it quickly. Put your mind to finishing even if it takes a week. While you are concentrating on finishing you can forget other things."

"Yes, I like to finish anything I start so I will give it a try."

Christmas was approaching and Sheila had no idea what she would do. Len had the solution. He had ordered a live turkey from the butcher. Twelve live turkeys had been ordered from Edmonton and Len had his name booked for one. Ralph's Native Canadian friend would kill the turkey and prepare it for roasting. The man would take the innards, feet, neck and head, of course the feathers. Ralph was so excited; he had not had turkey for years. He had ordered a leg of pork which they could have at New Year's Eve. Rhonda would cook the turkey and prepare Christmas puddings. Sheila asked what she could do and was told to help Rhonda with the Christmas puddings. Now she had a new interest other than the jigsaws.

Sheila was learning to cook but she did not cook cakes or puddings. Pudding making was a joyous occasion and a time to sample Ralph's wines. Jigsaw puzzles, exercising in her flat and pudding making were making her life easier. The weather was really cold, and she was very happy to get rides to and from work and the shops. The library was close enough to walk in her snowshoes but it was a struggle. The librarian asked several times whether she should call a friend to pick her up. Sheila was adamant that she would make it home as it was part of her exercise. She was now doing two jigsaws a week and getting good at finding pieces. Work was easy and she was looking into the records. She visited the workshop and got to know the employees. They all had interesting stories and seemed to be of various nationalities. There were several East Europeans and a couple of Germans, they were all happy to live in Yellowknife.

Christmas Eve was a happy time and Rhonda said they could all sleep at her place. The only problem was they only had a single car garage so Len's car had to be taken home so he could plug in his heater. Ralph would bring him back so his car could be plugged into the power supply. Sheila had the second bedroom with a double bed and Len slept on the couch. Sheila felt sorry for Len but would not give up her double bed.

The turkey was a large one and sufficient for Boxing Day and several days after. Sheila had to restrict her eating as the Christmas pudding was delicious, and Rhonda had made minced pies which she could not resist. They had a short break from each other and then it was New Year's Eve. There was a dance at the dance hall, but Ralph advised against it as it could get rowdy and sometimes violent. Len told that Russian New Year was the most important holiday. This was the best time for celebration but there would always be problems as many people would get drunk. The religious holiday for Christmas was later in January, but he had never been in a church except when he lived with his aunt and that was a small church, he thought the service was boring.

The leg of pork was cooked just right and roast potatoes with apple sauce went down a treat. Rhonda had made the apple sauce in the summer and had also stored the potatoes from her garden. Rhonda was an expert at preserving and pickling, she explained that it was necessary with the long winters. Len was reminiscing about pickled cabbage and cucumbers his mother would store. At midnight they all sang Auld Lang Syne. Even Len knew the words and along with the radio they gave a lusty rendition. At the end of the song everyone kissed. Sheila was wondering whether she would get a long kiss from Len, but he did not take advantage of the situation. Sheila was a bit disappointed.

Sheila was starting to regret telling Len she was not interested in romance; she should have waited to understand Len. He was a perfect boss and gentleman; he was always available to give help. She could not imagine her life in Yellowknife without him. Life without Len in this town could have been much more difficult and without Rhonda and Ralph it would have been impossible.

Early in February they went ice fishing again and when she caught her first fish, she gave Len a long hug; even Ralph noticed. Later in the month the weather started to warm, many days it was only -20C so they decided to go on a hunt. This was a long-distance hunt and Ralph was about to give up when the local trackers spied a herd. Ralph said he would shoot a big buck and if he missed and the buck ran to the left Sheila would have a shot. If the buck ran to the right Len would shoot. Ralph reminded Sheila this would be a moving target and the buck was pointed in her direction. If the buck ran straight away, they could all shoot.

The suspense was killing Sheila, she was quite tired after the trek but now she was wide awake, the adrenaline kicked in. Ralph shot, hit the buck but it did about face and Len killed it. Sheila did not shoot but ran to Len and gave him a long kiss. The local trackers were smiling but did not laugh. This was a large male, and it took all of them to drag it to the truck. Sheila was pulling her weight and one of the locals said she should rest. Later Ralph told her she had impressed his friends and she was invited to a dance when the weather was warmer. Ralph told her not to worry she would not have to dance but watch the men dance.

Ralph had persuaded Len to hire a couple of young Native Canadians to work in the workshop.

They were eager to learn and when Sheila came to the workshop and helped Ralph to set up a piece on the lathe they were speechless. Ralph explained that they called her super lady, and they would look for wives like her. Ralph said that it could be an impossible task. Sheila gave him a weak punch on the shoulder while laughing. She was thinking that this desolate place had introduced her to things she could not have seen previously and dear friends.

In spring Len asked for her help. He had invited his younger sister to visit in the summer but his flat was not well furnished and he needed a woman's touch to buy new furniture. Sheila had never been to Len's flat and when she went she realized he did indeed have almost no furniture. Almost everything would have to be shipped in by rail from Edmonton. Len had catalogues from two furniture companies and needed help making a choice. The first item was a bed. Single beds were not much cheaper than a double bed and Sheila said as it would be summer his sister might be cooler in a double bed. Len was thinking this woman thinks differently. He had a serviceable table, but the chairs were old and rickety. There was only one armchair which was also old.

"This furniture could cost a lot of dollars and then there is freight."

"Don't worry I spend very little of my income. Freight will cost nothing as we have a container for the mine every month and it is never full. I want my sister to be comfortable for three months, probably the first time in her life."

That phrase put a smile on Sheila's face. She had really misjudged Len when she first arrived and now, she was regretting her warning.

His sister Ludmila, called Mila, was studying chemistry at university and Len had a Canadian student work visa lined up if Russia would let her out. His case to the Canadians had been a good one; the Yukon received very few student work visas. Mila had obtained a passport which was a good sign. The university had approved now it was up to the relevant authorities. Len had no idea of the procedure, but his elder sister Olga was helping Mila and if anyone could bully the authorities it was Olga. Sheila had never seen Len worried and so preoccupied with this problem. He had booked a ticket from Moscow to Toronto on Aeroflot and then Air Canada to Edmonton. He would meet Mila in Edmonton and fly with her to Yellowknife. He was investing a lot of money in this trip and Sheila was excited to meet this sister.

Finally word came that everything had been approved. Len wanted to celebrate, and Ralph and Rhonda said they would pick up Sheila and bring her to his flat. Rhonda would drive so Ralph could have a drink. He had ordered in food and there was vodka, whisky and beer. He also had Champagne, soft drinks and a bottle of white wine for the ladies. One of his Italian workers had advised him about the wine. The food was mainly Chinese as they were good at delivering food.

Finally Mila was on the way. Sheila saw an excited Len; he could talk of nothing else. Sheila had no sisters or brothers, but she wondered if she would be so excited if they were coming. Len flew to Edmonton to pick up his sister, he explained he did not want her to get lost. That amused Sheila.

Sheila, Rhonda and Ralph were waiting at the airport to greet them. They had flowers as Len told them that was a normal Russian greeting. Rhonda said it first.

"She is beautiful, she looks like a film star."

Sheila was nodding approval and on Len's arm they looked like a happy couple. Sheila was not sure what she was expecting but this girl surpassed anything she had in her mind. Len introduced everyone and Mila tried her best to say their names. Ralph said Len's sister was the most beautiful girl he had ever seen.

"Yes, in the airport everyone was looking at us I suppose they thought Mila was my girlfriend."

"You should be so lucky."

Len was not sure what Sheila meant but he just smiled. Sheila was wondering why she had said it, she would have to think before speaking in future. Probably she had said it because she had been confronted by a beautiful girl on Len's arm.

Len took Sheila aside and asked if she would help Mila with spoken English. He had expected her to speak better English as she had lessons at school and university. She did not get any spoken English in Moscow and Sheila could take some time off from work.

"I have no problem, but I will do my job and teach at the same time; the office is a good place with Rhonda and I."

At Len's flat he produced bread, salt and vodka. Mila asked for water, no vodka. He had ordered food and hoped his sister liked Chinese food. She said she had never tried Chinese, but she liked the rice. Len took Sheila aside and said he did not know what she ate or drink.

"Ask her what she likes, you can ask her in English then in Russian."

"You are so smart, why did I not think of that?"

"Because you are in a happy state and can't think straight."

Both Rhonda and Sheila noticed that Mila was wearing thick clothing and although this was early June, she would need a bit lighter blouses and skirts. These two ladies were now in discussion as how to dress this model. Mila came from the bedroom and asked if that was her bed. Of course she asked in Russian and then Len repeated the question in English. Mila said she would get lost in such a big bed. After translation they were all laughing. Len told Sheila that the bed was a master stroke, a phrase he had learnt from Sheila.

Len was warned that the next day, a Friday the office would be empty, Sheila and Rhonda were taking Mila shopping. Len was insistent that anything they spent on Mila was his shout. The first place they went was Rhonda's house where there was a good breakfast. Rhonda was proud to show Mila her preserved food. Mila said with some difficulty that her mother would make preserves in the summer. They leant that winter in Moscow could be as cold as Yellowknife but generally only for a short time. Next it was shopping for clothes. There was not much choice, but Mila liked bright clothes. After buying a couple of skirts it was back to Rhonda's place for lunch. Rhonda had cheese, pickles, cooked meat and of course bread and butter. Mila tucked into the bread and butter then sampled the cheese and meat. Sheila and Rhonda observed what she liked. Mila said the butter was the best and she loved bread. The coffee she thought was a bit strong, but she took it without milk or sugar.

Later they went grocery shopping. The first place was the butcher. Mila started to cry; Rhonda asked her the problem. Mila asked what would happen to all this meat she had never seen so much. Sheila explained it would go in the freezer for the next day. Mila wanted to know why people were not flooding the shop to buy meat. Sheila said it would be there tomorrow and they probably had enough meat at home.

"We never have enough meat, and the butcher runs out before lunch. We queue every day for meat."

Sheila thought about that statement it was giving her the shivers.

Mila was composed when they entered the supermarket and she was just amazed at what was available. Rhonda noticed she was looking at the salami and sausages, so they bought some sliced salami and a good ring of sausages. They bought milk and yoghurt and Mila asked for kefir but there was none, and anyway, Sheila did not know what it was. They bought plenty of food and they could stock Len's fridge. They finally dropped Mila at Len's flat, and they all agreed it was fun shopping.

The next day being Saturday they all met for lunch at Rhonda's place. She had barbecued sausages and marinated venison, there was also plenty of bread and butter. Rhonda dug up some potatoes and they were put on the barbecue. They were small potatoes as this was early in the summer. Mila tried some of Ralph's wine and she enjoyed it. He had picked a slightly sweeter wine and told Len she might prefer a sweeter wine than a dryer wine. Len was not a wine drinker and needed all the help he could get.

The next few weeks in the office were fun and Rhonda was putting in more hours. Sheila took Mila to the workshop and the men were transfixed. She jokingly told one of the men that Mila was a film star and it went around the workshop like fire, and they all believed it. Len had arranged for a salary for Mila and said she would not spend a cent; she would go home with more money than she had ever seen. There was a crude laboratory at the mine site and Mila visited it several times. All the miners were mesmerized by this film star. Mila started to look at the mine process and the assays of the ores.

At the next management meeting Mila was introduced as a chemist on a student work visa. At this meeting Sheila did a lot more talking. She showed that although the mine was making a profit the ore was getting thinner, with Mila nodding approval. On the other hand the workshop was making more money and getting a reputation for good work. The manager said very little except he was very pleased with the meeting. After the manager had gone Sheila told Len they had slayed him. Len asked about to slay but he said the manager could not take his eyes off Mila. Sheila had to admit Mila had the same effect on her.

Three months passed with Sheila and Mila in contact every day. Mila's English improved daily, and she was soon a better speaker than Len; she was a very quick learner. Rhonda had learnt to make *pirashki* and *pilmeni* and Mila had learnt to make Yorkshire pudding, pizza and rice pudding. Len could not believe the change in his sister.

Mila had told them stories about life in Moscow, Sheila started to pick up Russian words. She also started to see differences in the languages. Jokes were not always easy to translate and also understood. Everyday living was different and family life was different. Mila's elder sister worked as a physicist in a secret establishment and none of her colleagues knew about Len. They only knew she had a sister at university studying chemistry. They were proud of Len, but he was never mentioned outside the family. Mila had visited her father, but he had taken up with another woman. She learnt that her mother had divorced him to keep the Moscow flat. Her father was not unfriendly but told her to go back to Moscow. Her aunt, her father's elder sister had been much more welcoming.

Time was up for Mila's visit and Sheila felt like she was losing a sister. Len took Mila to Edmonton after a lot of crying at the airport. Ralph even made the comment he wished he had had a sister like her. Rhonda said she would love a sister like Mila. Sheila was thinking could she have her as a sister. At the airport Mila told Sheila before leaving that her brother was good husband material. Sheila was thinking the same.

Sheila was crying as they left the airport and confided in Rhonda that she he never felt such affection for another woman. She wished she had a sister to compare the feeling.

"Maybe your love for Len is involved. " Rhonda said her piece and left it at that.

Life in Yellowknife was very good in the summer and early fall, but winter was approaching. Mila was very much missed and often her name came up in conversation. Sheila was now better prepared for the coming winter. Len sprang a surprise; he had been offered a job in a coal mine near Edmonton owned by the owners of the gold mine in Yellowknife. He had asked whether Sheila could go as his secretary otherwise if she would not go, he would turn down the job.

"We are a team, and I would not go anywhere without you."

Sheila was overwhelmed and of course said yes. He told her initially it was to manage the workshops with a possibility of managing the whole mine. They would each have a flat and the pay would be better. Sheila was wondering how she would have reacted to a shared flat, she could only dream. The management meeting earlier in the summer had impressed a senior partner. He had recommended the offer to Len and Sheila.

Rhonda and Ralph were not happy, but Len had recommended Ralph take over the workshop and Rhonda to work full time if she wanted. Len suggested he, Sheila and Ralph sit down and run through the workings of the workshop and particularly the paperwork. They would only be a phone call away and it was a company phone. Len said he had some furniture to sell but anything Rhonda wanted she could have. Their final dinner was both happy and sad. Ralph promised they would try to get to Edmonton. A couple of Ralph's Native Canadian friends stopped by to say the couple would be missed and to wish them luck. Sheila had been to a couple of their dances and was treated like royalty.

Sheila and Len travelled by train to Edmonton as they had a lot of luggage. Sheila could not believe how much 'stuff' she had accumulated in just over a year. Luggage was no problem as in Edmonton they were picked up by a mine lorry. They sat in the front seat with the driver and Sheila was enjoying the close contact with Len. The mine was on the northern edge of Edmonton and winter could be as cold as in Yellowknife. Their flats were adjacent in a company owned building. Sheila was thinking that this could be almost as good as sharing a flat. Len's car had come by train, and they were immediately mobile. Sheila had not been in Edmonton and Len showed her the bits he knew, which were not very many. Sheila realized this was a big city with lots of shops. She was not really a shopper but had to try this new experience not available in Yellowknife. The houses were different from Yellowknife, and she started to have an interest in real estate.

Both flats were furnished but Sheila though immediately about improvements. Len was wondering how he was going to fit the furniture from Yellowknife into this new apartment. The next day they went to the office which was in a building next to the mine. Sheila realized this mine was very different to the gold mine. Len's office was next to the manager's office and big enough to have a desk for Sheila. The manager, Roger, was a Scot and he had lost nothing of his accent. Sheila had no difficulty, but Len was struggling with this new accent. Roger was very happy that Sheila had shorthand and asked if he could borrow her occasionally to take letters. He had to write what he wanted for the typists but now he could just talk. He could not stand the Dictaphone. Sheila said she was happy to help Roger anyway she could. The workshop was quite small but the warehouse with old and new equipment was large. Len was responsible for maintenance and repair of equipment. Sheila was quickly on to a scheme to manage all these duties and expand the workshop to make new parts. Len realized she was the real manager; he was just the figurehead (another word learnt from Sheila).

Work at the mine was nonstop through the winter, the only problem was keeping the surface services working. Coal was coming to the surface all year round and it had to be shipped out continually. The temperature at the surface was often -30centigrade and machinery could break down under the stress of the temperature. Len realized this job was harder than his last, but Sheila was such a help. Roger was so happy to have Sheila around and he invited Len and Sheila to several dinners. Mary, Roger's wife liked Sheila and a new friendship was formed.

Sheila wanted to be closer to Len and they had several intimate sessions, but they never ended in intercourse. Ralph and Rhonda were going to visit, and Sheila suggested that they could stay in her flat and she would sleep with Len.

Len had been playing it cool but now he was excited. He loved Sheila from the first but always remembered her warning about romance. His first impulse was to try to take her to bed but this lady was different, and he did not want to spoil his chances; he had restrained himself. Now she had suggested what he wanted all along. He had observed the effect Mila had on Sheila. He did not realize his love of Mila was the greatest influence on Sheila. Sheila saw a lonely family man who wanted to be reunited with his family. That was good husband material.

Ralph and Rhonda had only passed through Edmonton, many years ago, on their way to Yellowknife. They were excited to see the big city. On their tour Ralph could not get over the large shopping centre. He was most interested in a hardware store that seemed to have every tool imaginable. Len was telling him to buy anything he wanted and put it on the company account. Rhonda was interested in the women's clothing shops, most of the clothes were entirely unsuitable for Yellowknife but good to look at.

Sheila was telling her some of the lighter dresses might be wearable a couple of times a year.

Len ordered take away from a Chinese and an Italian restaurant and they all enjoyed the evening meal with plenty of drinks. Ralph and Rhonda were telling Len how much they enjoyed working with each other. With an increase in salary they would be ordering a turkey at Christmas; that caused a lot of laughter. When the sleeping arrangements were discussed, Rhonda looked quizzically at Sheila who smiled. Neither Ralph nor Len seemed to notice, if they did they did not comment.

Sheila could not wait till the other couple left and she had Len alone. Earlier she had brought her pyjamas to Len's flat, but she was hoping she would not need them. As soon as Rhonda and Ralph left, and they shut the door Len was being kissed and hugged very tightly. Sheila was pressing her body up against him and it was having an exciting effect.

"I am not a virgin."

"Neither am I so let's see what we have forgotten with time."

Sheila could not think why she had that outburst, but it had done the trick. Off they went to the bedroom, and it was all so quick; they were both excited. There was little foreplay and both climaxed. As they lay together Len said that next time they should take it easy. Sheila replied that she was ready for next time now! Len said he needed to relax, and they fell asleep in each other's arms.

The next two days with Ralph and Rhonda were very happy times and the night times were happier. Ralph discussed his work and received advice mainly from Sheila. Rhonda wanted to come back again to do more shopping. After their friends went back to Yellowknife Len and Sheila settled into married life without the license. Sheila wanted to get married in England, but she wanted Mila as a bridesmaid. Len said that it would be too difficult to get Mila to England and she was now working for a state agency. Her sister Olga was working for a secret organization as a physicist. Sheila had educated in-laws but that meant they had more restrictions.

They sent photos to Moscow, but the return mail had bad news. Len's mother had died and that had a profound effect on Len. He suddenly went very quiet and excused himself from work for three days. Sheila was able to handle any problems and she kept Len at 'arms-length'. Len explained that he needed to see visions of his mother and to tell her about his life journey. He also had to think about his father and talk to him. Although Sheila did not really understand she had to let Len have space to grieve. He only drank water and ate bread for three days. On the fourth day he went back to his normal routine and apologized to Sheila for his behaviour. She said she understood although she was not sure whether she did.

The events were playing on Sheila's mind, so she suggested they go to Russia using Intourist. Len said it was impossible as they might throw him in jail for not doing his service in the army. Len said that Sheila should go and meet his sisters. She was thinking this was very different, she would get married and have a solo honeymoon to meet her in laws. The plans for the wedding were all made by Sheila, and they would be married in a registry office. Once they were married Sheila would take a trip with Intourist to Russia. By this time Len was manager of the mine and Sheila an indispensable secretary.

They journeyed to England and Len was introduced to his future in laws. They were a bit skeptical about their future son-in-law, but Len kissed his future mother-in-law's hand and gave his future father-in-law a strong hug and a bottle of expensive whisky. Now everyone was happy. Sheila contacted some of her old friends but not her former boyfriend. Her friends were amazed at her new life.

They were married with Len having no friends and his best man was the husband of one of Sheila's friends. There was an absent bridesmaid, but Sheila had a photo of Mila on a stand. That photo was of great interest with the guests. After a short honeymoon, at a hotel in Worcester, Sheila was off to Russia. Len stayed with his in laws who were enjoying his company. At the pub, the patrons were all enjoying his stories especially about ice fishing. He did not like the local beer, but he found a cold lager he enjoyed. Len was finding some of the local dialect a bit difficult, but he became a good smiler and nodder. His stories about his escape from Russia had all the pub patrons interested and he was invited to talk to a local group.

Sheila was to spend two days in Moscow then a week in Sochi followed by three days in Leningrad. On the first day the flight landed at Sheremetyevo and the tourists were transported to the hotel by coach. Sheila had seen Mila in the crowd and told her they were staying in the Cosmos Hotel, but she would make her own way to see her two sisters. As the bus took them to the hotel Sheila was very interested in the sights. There seemed to be a lot of buildings, but they all needed a paint job. She was to stay in a hotel and a city tour was planned the next day, which she declined. She had her relative's address in English and Russian and directions to the Metro. Getting into the metro was interesting and she was on the longest escalator she had ever seen. Mila had taught her some Cyrillic script which came in useful. The only problem was that she had to change trains at a major interchange station. She could sort of read the Cyrillic script but after two tours of the station she had to ask directions from a policeman. When he saw the address, he escorted her to the correct platform and told her he was happy to help her. She had counted the stations and could also read the map in the train. She alighted at the correct station but now where to go. She asked some workmen, but they seemed to be from Eastern Russia and could not understand her. Finally she found a policeman who escorted her to a block of flats. He was very glad to give her assistance. Maybe this state was a bit repressive but so far, the police had shown that people could be different than the country where they lived.

Mila was sitting on the balcony, and she watched Sheila approach. When she realized it was Sheila, she gave out a shriek. Mila rushed to meet Sheila and there was a lot of hugging and tears, mainly from Mila. Mila thanked the policeman who was smiling. Len's sisters had known Sheila was visiting but not exactly the timing. Olga was still at work but that gave Sheila and Mila time to acquaint. Mila prepared some snacks including *pirashki* that Len had described. These were with potatoes and cabbage. Len had told Sheila the best contained meat.

Olga arrived and there were plenty of introductions. Olga's English was not anywhere as good as Mila's, but Sheila could tell who was boss. She was just watching this interaction and tried to analyse it. Olga had to pick up her son Maxim and Mila explained they could all go together, or they would let Olga go alone. Sheila wanted to go and meet her nephew. Sheila now saw a young Len. Back in the flat Mila was presented with her bridesmaid dress and Maxim was dancing with joy. Olga was also admiring the dress and Sheila was wondering why she had not made both her sisters brides' maids. Sheila was upset she had not brought anything for Maxim, but Mila said to buy him something later. Mila escorted Sheila to her hotel and explained they would not let her in the hotel; it was for foreigners and special ladies.

The next day Mila and Sheila spent a time walking by the river and seeing the Kremlin. Olga was going to get to Leningrad, but Mila would try her best to get to Sochi. In the hotel Sheila was thinking about her new sisters. She was an only child and now she had a family. Her elder sister was so different from Mila but that was as it should be. The only problem was that she was experiencing all this without Len. She was wondering how they could all live in their small flat.

It was summer and Sochi was very warm, and Sheila decided she would buy Maxim summer clothes. Before Mila arrived, Sheila was approached on the street and offered money for her jeans and sandals. Later Mila explained that western clothes could be resold at a good price. This was all foreign to Sheila. Mila explained that summer clothes for Maxim might be of limited use and a Russian flag, and the Union Jack would capture his imagination. Sheila searched and found a Canadian flag, now she had a present. Mila later reported that Maxim said it was the best present he had ever received. Sheila recognized this was a different culture, she had a glimpse when she talked to Mila, but she was now experiencing it and it was strange.

After the short stay in Sochi the tour group was flown to Leningrad. Sheila arrived at the place she knew as Saint Petersburg and in the afternoon and was greeted by Olga. Olga was trying her best English and it was much better than Sheila's Russian. Sheila booked into the hotel and then they were off to see the old city. They had a meal at a café where the food was okay, but the coffee was terrible. Then Olga was showing her the sights, they seemed to walk for miles. This was June, the time of the white nights and it was light until nearly midnight. Finally at eleven p.m., Sheila apologized because she was tired. Olga understood, this sister was used to an easy life.

When Sheila flew out of Russia, she felt she had lost something. Back in England Sheila recounted all her experiences. Len was particularly interested with her opinion of his sisters and Maxim. She described Maxim as a young Len and there were tears streaming down his face. He was laughing when Sheila told him Olga was a force. Mila was not yet married and was as beautiful as ever. Len asked if was possible she would be comfortable for them living with his family. Sheila said she would try her best to have all of them together.

Several years passed and the mine was making lots of money. They had bought a three-bedroom house. Under Sheila's guidance the machine shop had become a money spinner and the company bosses were very happy. The only problem was that Sheila could not get pregnant. Len had been checked out and there was no problem. Sheila also seemed to be fertile. She could see that Len was blaming himself, but she reassured him his sperm count was good and it would happen when it happened. He really wanted children.

Life in Russia was changing under Gorbachev and Yeltsin. Len and his sisters were able to meet up in Belgrade. Sheila had made all the arrangements but had to hold the fort in Canada. Len was a wreck when he returned; he could not stop talking about his sisters but particularly about his nephew. Sheila realized he was missing a son. The only thing she could do was to look at adoption.

Then a long for long forgotten dream came true. Olga, Mila and Maxim were allowed to visit for three weeks. Mila had been in Yellowknife, but Edmonton was different. Len and Sheila decided to meet them in Toronto and have a couple of days sightseeing. Len had only passed through Toronto and Sheila had only seen the train station. They decided to take a city tour and a harbour cruise and stay in a good hotel.

They all met at the airport and after the initial greetings Len suggested they have a coffee before going to the hotel. He wanted everyone to relax and particularly himself. They were sitting for a short time and then Olga noticed Maxim was not with them; he had wandered off. Olga started to panic, and Mila was telling Sheila that Len was telling her not to worry, he would go to the information counter, and they would broadcast in English and Russian. Just as Len was about to leave for the information desk, Maxim strolled back. Olga grabbed him and hugged him very tightly he even protested. He wanted Uncle Len to come with him. Sheila was seeing motherly love as she had little experience with young children. Len returned laughing. Maxim had shown him a notice that said Test and Maxim thought they might test his English. It was a place where they did medical tests.

Olga was overwhelmed by the hotel; it was so spacious and the bathroom was a delight. They checked in and went for a stroll near the hotel. Maxim wanted a hamburger, so their evening meal was hamburger and chips at a local restaurant. Of course Maxim could not finish his large hamburger, so Olga helped him. Sheila was getting a short course in motherhood.

The city tour was a good introduction to Canada and the harbour tour was enjoyed by everyone but particularly Maxim. The flight to Edmonton was entertaining, Len allowed Maxim and Olga to both have window seats. Len sat next to Maxim and the whole flight consisted of questions and answers.

Olga could not get over the shops even though Mila had warned her. Maxim was the star. They were playing with a ball and Maxim kicked Len in the shin and then trying to get a ball he punched Len in the face. Len had to retire to weep; he explained to Sheila that those blows were something special. Olga was a dominant force, but Sheila loved her approach to everything. Olga was in long conversations with Len, and she was telling him what to do. Sheila was watching with amusement as her husband had to take advice from another woman. Mila was Mila and just loved everything, shopping with Mila was a delight. Mila was so good looking she was attracting lots of potential suitors, and this amused Sheila.

It was time for them to leave and after the trio left to go back to Moscow Sheila said they should discuss adoption. Len realized she had the right idea, but adoption was foreign to him. A long discussion had him positive about adoption. Sheila was collecting all the details when she missed a period. She had thought she was too old to get pregnant. Without Len knowing she did the pregnancy test, and it was positive. She visited the doctor, and he told her to relax and wait as false positives were not uncommon. Her hopes were very high, and a false positive was unthinkable. Sheila was a calm person, but this was causing her to feel stressed. She was dying to tell Len but if it was false, she was not sure how he would take the news. She wondered whether it could have happened when her sisters were visiting. Maybe seeing Olga and Maxim interacting had made her relax.

Time passed and she had an ultrasound that showed a tiny foetus. Now she could tell Len. He looked at her in disbelief when she told him, he was not familiar with ultrasound. Then it hit him they were going to have a child, he danced around the room. He also realized that Sheila had to take it easy, and he made her sit down. Sheila was laughing at his reaction. Len wanted her to give up work, but she explained if she had to stay at home she would be much stressed and that could cause a miscarriage. Now Len was out of his depth and decided to listen to his wife.

They agreed that Len would need an assistant manager. After consulting the owners Len appointed a young fellow who had been injured in the mine and was now working on the surface. Sheila thought it a good choice and sat down with this young man to tell him about the workings of the mine. She stressed that machine maintenance was most important and told him to study the workshop and the maintenance warehouse. She told him that when he went down to the workings to look for problems and how they could be fixed. Len was keen for Sheila to sit in the office and was happy she had new eyes and ears.

News from Moscow was that everything seemed to be changing. Len was keen to make a move when the system relaxed. He was in touch with Politian's from the Yukon and Alberta. He was telling them that many Russians were well educated and had skills needed in Canada. Using his family as examples was having a positive effect. Sheila was happy with the way he could talk to people; she always knew that it was his strength. She was surprised when a Federal MP invited Len to Ottawa to talk to some of his colleagues. Len was nervous but Sheila told him to be himself and answer any questions truthfully. On returning Len was full of stories and his favourite was when he had an audience applauded his speech. He told them he escaped when he was young, and his sisters got the education and he got Canada.

Sheila's pregnancy was going very well, and Len finally saw photos of the foetus. He was very emotional at seeing these images. Sheila told him he could listen to the baby. He pressed his ear to her stomach and Sheila could feel the tears on her stomach. She had a very emotional husband. They went to prenatal classes, and they were the oldest couple, that threw Len for a while but he soon made friends with the young couples. One nurse asked if he would witness the delivery. He said no as he was too emotional and would get in the way. Finally Sheila was persuaded to stay at home, but Len's assistant would often visit with ideas and news from the mine. Sheila had a lot of time and effort expended in this mine and she was happy to receive any news.

Sheila had rather a long labour of several hours and Len was a nervous wreck. His assistant was telling him Sheila was a strong lady and not to worry. This young fellow called Chuck was almost a member of the family. Finally the baby was delivered, and she was a girl. Len was introduced to his daughter and burst into tears. Sheila said she was sorry it was not a son, but she did not want to go through that ordeal again.

"I am not worried about a son, but the sight of this tiny baby suddenly had me thinking about my mother, she would never see her granddaughter. Maybe we think differently but I am so happy to have a daughter."

"We don't think differently because I know you are always thinking about family."

Sheila wanted to name her daughter Mila, but Len intervened and asked if they could call her Larrisa, his mother's second name. Sheila had no argument as there was already one Mila in the family. Len was almost afraid to hold Larrisa she was so small. The hospital kept mother and daughter for a couple of days for observation. Len was taking plenty of photos of mother and daughter to send to Moscow. He could not wait to get them home; he was lonely in their house alone.

At home Sheila was interested in taking care of her baby but wanted news of the mine constantly; it was like her second baby. Larrisa was starting to grow, and Len was always playing with her. His face lit up whenever she was around. Sheila was in constant correspondence with Mila. News was coming from Moscow that the Soviet Union was collapsing, and Yeltsin was taking over Russia. Len sensed this was the time, so he sent messages to his sisters to go to the

Canadian Embassy and apply for immigration. He would send affidavits from important people and promise his financial support. A few weeks passed and their visas were approved. Len sent them tickets and hoped there would be no problem in Moscow. There was some confusion in Moscow, but they were allowed to leave.

Olga had not resigned her position but at the airport she sent a resignation letter siting family problems but omitting her escape to Canada. This was only Olga's second long flight, and she was nervous but Mila was constantly telling her to relax. Part of her nervousness was due to the fact they would not return. Maxim loved the flights, but he was asleep for long periods. Mila was living a new dream whether she was awake or asleep. Changing planes in Toronto Mila took charge. It was not a first as they had done it before, but this time Olga was in a sort of trance. She was still worried about leaving Russia and now she was contemplating a new life.

The greetings at Edmonton airport were a very happy but a teary occasion. Even Sheila was shedding tears, Maxim and Larrisa probably wondered what all the fuss was about. Back at the house there was a party. Ralph and Rhonda had come from Yellowknife and Chuck was there. He could not take his eyes off Mila.

"Sorry Chuck she is too old for you, but I am sure you will find a good-looking wife as you are a good looking fellow."

"Sheila she is the most beautiful lady I have ever seen I can't imagine finding one like her."

"Find one who loves you no matter how she looks."

Ralph and Rhonda were very happy to see Mila and were introduced to Olga. Len was playing with Maxim and Larrisa. Sheila was looking at the group and marvelling at her life. She had left Birmingham angry, had gone to the ends of the earth and now she had a big happy Russian family.

Brummie orphans in Quebec

Alistair (called Ally) was seven years old attending Barford Road Infants School. He was a very happy gregarious boy. He had joined the school at five years of age just as the war started. Now all the boys in his class were his mates. They kicked anything kickable in the school yard and in the street, preferably a ball but it could be a stone or a bit of wood. His long socks were always around his ankles and his shorts showed his skinny legs. With his shirt hanging out of his pants he looked just like most of the boys in his area. He was supposed to wear a cap to school, but it was never on straight and neither was his tie. His mother was continually telling him he was a scruff.

In class he was one of the brighter pupils. He was always putting up his hand to answer questions. Ally always wanted to be first and was very disappointed when beaten to the answer, particularly by a girl. He was good at arithmetic and had a mastery of fractions which seemed to evade some of his mates. Ally was rarely in trouble except one time when he went with one of his mates at lunchtime to his mate's house. They were not to leave the school premises at lunchtime, and he was soon missed. When they returned a teacher sent them to the headmaster. There was no punishment only a stern talking to.

Ally lived with his parents in a small house, he was an only child. The house was two storey with two bedrooms. The front door opened on to the street and Ally's mom was always scrubbing the front step and keeping the pavement clean. There was a small back yard, and the toilet and coal house were in the back garden. There was no bathroom, and a large tin bath was used once a week. Ally was lucky he had his own bedroom, many of his mates had to share bedrooms and even beds.

Ally's father was Scottish, and his mother was from London. They had both run away from home and had met in Birmingham. They were married and not long after had Ally. Ally's father, Jo, worked in a factory making brass parts for munitions. He had been exempted from call-up due to his job. He worked on nights and was in control of the whole factory. Ally's mother Doris worked in a school canteen but not Barford Road School. Ally would go to school and come home to an empty house. If it was raining, he would go to a neighbour otherwise he would play in the street.

Rationing was causing some families problems, but Ally's family did not have many problems as Doris was a good adventurous cook. She had found that the railway embankments were good for finding all sorts of herbs including horseradish. She would take Ally out picking at the weekends. Ally would have preferred to be playing football in the street, but he did appreciate tasty food.

Ally knew almost nothing of his grandparents, they were not even on his parents wedding photo. There was one relative on the photo, a young man who was best man. His father told him that was his younger brother Jock, uncle Jock. Jock had visited once, and Ally could hardly understand a word he said. He was a handsome bloke in a kilt and was very well built and Ally had to look up at him.

Most of his mates had family in the local area, there were uncles and aunts living in the same street or only one or two streets away. Ally envied them, they had plenty of cousins and he had none. He was invited to many family parties and wondered if his parents were missing all these gatherings. Jo and Doris were quite comfortable to be alone, they were in love.

Like most of his mates he was sent to Sunday school so the parents could have a quiet Sunday afternoon. He did agree to join the choir, but he hated learning scriptures off by heart. His parents rarely went to church but did come occasionally when he sang in the choir. He enjoyed singing in church but almost slept through sermons.

The bombing had started when he was in the second class. The school had an air raid shelter and there was always excitement when the siren sounded. The children were trouped into the shelter and the noise of excited children often drowned out the noise of the bombing. The teachers had a problem getting their pupils back in class and ready to work after the all-clear. The school was less than half a mile from a group of factories. With a canal and a railway line close by this area was a prime target for German bombers.

Like all young boys he wanted to see where the bombs dropped. One stray bomb had hit a house near the park and a crowd of excited children had gathered near the site, they were being restrained by fire wardens. The bomb had landed in the garden and all that was visible was a big hole. This was the subject of conversation for a week. Ally talked to one of the wardens who told him it was only a matter of time before a bomb landed on houses. This neighbourhood was too close to factories.

Ally's father was a foreman on nights at a local factory and was always in contact with the local defence force and the fire wardens. Much of the machinery in the factory could not be shut down but he had to get the workers to the shelters. There were very few workers on nights, but their safety was his primary duty. He was often on his own in the factory while the bombing was taking place. He had to shut down some machines and keep others running. Doris was always telling him to get a safer job. He joked that he would die in his bed and not give the Germans satisfaction.

Although some factories in the vicinity were hit his factory remained safe.

At school one afternoon well before leaving time a policeman came and asked to gather all pupils that lived in Ally's street. Ally was lined up with ten other children. They were all wondering why they were gathered but the policeman said nothing. There had been bombing earlier and they had only recently come from the shelter. They trouped to the corner of their street, and they stopped before they entered the street. The policeman called out Ally and told a fire warden to look after the other children and keep them from entering their street. The policeman took Ally's hand and led him around the corner into his street.

Ally saw the street filled with people. There were a lot of wardens and police as well as housewives. As they walked down the street, he was seeing a lot of rubble on the road in the distance. The policeman held his hand and had the other hand on Ally's shoulder. They came close to where Ally lived and there were bricks all over the road. They reached to where Ally lived and there was no house just a pile if bricks. Ally looked, blinked and looked again there was no house. He put his hands to his face but when he withdrew them there was still no house. Ally now broke down in tears. The policeman hugged him to his chest and told Ally there had been a direct hit on his house, several houses had been demolished by the same bomb.

"Where are my mom and dad?"

"We are looking for them, but they were not in the shelter. Where were they when you went to school?"

"Dad works nights and was in bed and mom does not work today so she would be with him. She gave me breakfast and I went to school with a kiss."

The policeman had to restrain his emotions and gave Ally a little black diary.

"Write your name and address in this book, write the names of your parents. Write their birthdays if you remember them. Write anything you feel or see because later when you are grown you can remember these things."

The policeman was fighting back tears.

"Thank you sir; I like to write."

"This lady, one of your neighbours, will take you in for tonight and maybe a few days more and give you a cup of tea. Please be a good boy and do what she tells you, I will see you tomorrow."

Ally went off with Mrs Mitchell, he knew her well, two of her sons were in the army. He drank his tea, but he was in a sort of trance, he did not know what was happening. He had only the clothes he stood in, but Mrs Mitchell found some of her son's old clothes. His dreams were full of his mother's face. He tried to talk to her, but she was not listening. In the morning Mrs Mitchell gave him breakfast and told him there would be no school, some people were coming to talk to him. Ally realized there was a problem and now he wanted to see his mother. The policeman and a child welfare officer came to talk to him; he had no idea who this woman was.

Finally the policeman told him his parents were in the house when the bomb dropped, and they were both dead. Ally heard nothing else everything went black. The news sent him into shock, and he lost all ability to speak. He just buried his face in his hands and cried. No one could console him he just collapsed on the bed and continued to cry.

News had filtered out and Ally's parents were found in the house in each other's arms. Now the women of the street united and wanted to give Ally as much as they could. Ally was presented with clothes, a small brown suitcase and best of all a ten-shilling note. Ally was still in shock and all he could say was thank you but the ten-shilling note was something that stirred his emotion. Most of the time he sat on his bed and spoke very little, he would not go outside. He was afraid of what he would see. His dreams were filled with his father and mother, they always had smiling faces.

After a few days a nurse came to take Ally to a home. Mrs Mitchell was crying as were several of the female neighbours, Ally was just quiet and did not resist as he was placed in the car. He was put in an orphan's home and in a dormitory with eight other children. His suitcase contained all his clothes but he kept his possession's close to his chests, his black diary and his ten-shilling note.

During the next few months Ally was almost silent, he rarely spoke and would obey instructions but nothing more. The policeman who had shown Ally the devastation had learnt that Ally had an uncle in a Scottish regiment. He had been found and was given a twenty-four-hour pass to talk to Ally. The police had a few photos resurrected from the bomb site which they gave to Jock. Jock was taken to the home and asked if he could help Ally.

Jock walked into the dormitory to see Ally sitting on his bed. Ally had his head bowed and did not see his uncle.

"Ally McGregor I am your uncle Jock, stand up straight I want to greet my nephew."

Ally stood up and rushed to hug his uncle. Jock was trying to hold back tears.

"Ally, you are a McGregor and have to be strong for your father and your ancestors. Your father and mother will be watching you from heaven and you will grow to be a big strong man. When this war has ended, I will be back to take you home. I have a few photos taken from your home. One is with your father's wedding, and I am there look after them I am looking young there. Always take care of your mates, that's what we McGregors do. I cannot stay as there is some big operation planned and I have to play the bagpipes for the troops. I'll be back when we have victory."

Ally did look after that photo; it was one of his three vital possessions. Jock told the policeman that his interaction with Ally was more difficult than facing the enemy; unfortunately Jock was killed at the D-Day landing.

Ally looked around and found one of the boys in the dormitory who was always crying. He was five years old and had lost both parents. Uncle Jock's talk had made Ally think about helping others. This boy was called Thomas, but Ally decided to call him Tommy. Ally talked to Tommy but at first did not get much response. He did notice that Tommy cried less often so he must be getting through. There was a garden in the back of the dormitory, and they could play in it after they were brought from school. A nurse took them to school every day and brought them back to the hostel in the afternoon. Tommy only wanted to kick balls; he was not interested in throwing balls. One morning Tommy woke Ally.

"Can you look at my bum? It itches and it feels like something is moving."

Ally woke everyone up. "Nurse, Tommy has worms."

"There is always one; come with me I will clean you up and give you some medicine. No one to go near Tommy's bed; I will have to strip it."

After a while Tommy came back with his face screwed up.

"I think that medicine is worse than the worms and I have to have more tomorrow."

This was a breakthrough as Tommy started to talk to Ally more often. The bombing continued for a while and then stopped. The bombing scared Ally but it sent Tommy into fits of crying that even Ally had a problem to control. The nurses told them that the war would end soon. Ally decided they should escape. One Saturday morning Ally and Tommy left the dormitory; Ally had planned the right time to disappear without being noticed. They knew the area well and could find places to hide. They had forgotten they would get hungry and where to sleep. Late in the afternoon they entered the police station.

"We want to give ourselves up; we have escaped from the dormitory. There is nowhere to go, and we are hungry. Tommy's house is not there, and my house has gone we can't sleep in the park so we came here."

"Well, would you like a cup of tea?"

"Yes please, both me and Tommy like milk and sugar."

"Sit there while I make the tea."

The policeman went into the back room laughing to himself. After tea the sergeant had a talk to them and found both were orphans, he was very sympathetic He called a young policeman and instructed him to take them back to the dormitory.

"Look after these adventurers I am sure we will see them again."

After they left the sergeant took several deep breaths to calm himself. There were a lot of orphans around but thank God his family was safe.

The war came to an end and the dormitory emptied leaving only Ally and Tommy. One of the nurses said they might be sent to Canada and Ally said his uncle would come to pick him up. They finally had to tell him his uncle had died on D Day. That sent Ally into a silence Tommy could not break. Ally sat and continually looked at the wedding photo. He looked from face to face, they were all dead, he would never see them again. Finally he recalled his uncle's words, now he would have three looking at him.

One day Tommy told Ally about his dream where his mom and dad were smiling at him. Suddenly Ally sought of woke up and told Tommy he had similar dreams.

"They can see me, but I can only see them in dreams; maybe that is one of the drawbacks of being dead," said Ally

"They can't hold me."

"Well that is another drawback."

Ally was back to his old self and he and Tommy would talk about their parents. The only problem was that Tommy had no photos: Ally decided to share his photos. Finally they were on their way to Canada. The nurse was in tears when they were taken away, these two boys never caused problems and she had come to love them. They were taken to New Street Station where they met several other children who were going to Canada. Ally went around and met them all even the girls. They were all orphans between five and ten years old. Most were from Birmingham but two were from Coventry. This bunch was all very quiet, but Ally saw all of them as friends and told them so. He said they would all be going across the Atlantic on a big ship so they should all get to know each other. One of the nurses had shown him some atlases and shown him how big Canada was compared with England. He now started telling the group they were going to a country much bigger than England. Tommy said he had seen the maps and Ally was telling them the truth.

At Liverpool they were all aghast at the size of the ship they would board. This was a troop ship carrying Canadian soldiers back to Canada. The troops were lined up on the dock, but Ally and his friends were first to board. Many of the soldiers were smiling at them and blowing them kisses. Ally gave them a salute back and now the troops were laughing. On board ship they were segregated from the troops and had a very spacious dormitory. There was a curtain between the boys and girls. On deck they had their own space, but Ally was able to talk to the troops and get chewing gum. He distributed the gum to his group but only a couple of the boys would talk to the troops. None of the girls would talk to the troops.

Up on deck they had a football and a couple of tennis balls but little else. The girls asked for a skipping rope and the troops found a rope from somewhere. Ally thanked them on behalf of the girls. He watched as grown men cried when they watched the kids play. They were cheering Tommy when he kicked the ball. Many of the soldiers were telling him to pick up the ball and kick it. Once he did, they were cheering. Tommy was telling Ally only the goalkeeper took the ball in his hands and kicked it. Ally found out that in Canadian Football everyone took the ball in his hands and kicked it. Ally was practicing throwing and he had a group of soldiers who appreciated his skill. Many of these soldiers had children and Ally found they had not seen their children for five years.

As they approached Canada the excitement grew, the children were keen to see land. The sights along the St. Lawrence were exciting and some of the soldiers were talking about this province called Quebec. They stopped at Quebec City where some of the soldiers disembarked. There was a piper to wish them farewell and Ally and all the children waved them goodbye. Ally remembered his Uncle Jock was a piper, so he stood at attention and saluted. Many of the soldiers saluted back. Then the ship was off to Montreal where they would all disembark. Ally and Tommy were to stay in Quebec, but all the others would go to Ontario. Ally and Tommy were assigned to a farm near Shawinigan in Quebec. This was an English-speaking part of Quebec although French speakers were in the majority.

Ally and Tommy had a ride in a bus and were taken to a farm. As they were city boys, they had no idea about farming. They were greeted by the farmer Frank, his wife Dora and the local vicar John. Frank was immediately telling them they would have to work to earn their keep. Dora was much nicer telling them about their meals and sleeping arrangements. The vicar was telling them about school where he was the school master. Frank had a loud voice, and he was obviously in charge.

Tommy was afraid of Frank; his father had never talked to him in a loud voice. Ally was telling Tommy he should be more afraid of the vicar as he was the school master. Actually Ally did not like Frank he could be a problem he always seemed angry. Dora was very friendly and was telling them her husband was angry as he had sent two sons to war and was only getting half a one back. Ally asked what she meant. She said her sons had decided to join the army and she had tried to dissuade them. It was their choice, but Frank wanted them to work the farm. The eldest one was killed but he was in heaven and was with God. Dora was a very religious mother. Her second son had his lower leg blown off, so she did not have to pray for him.

Most of Ally's chores were involved with the cows and pigs, Tommy looked after the chickens and enjoyed his chores. Ally learned to milk the cows and got to know each cow. There were the quiet ones and the problem ones. He tried to pass the problem ones to Dora. At first he thought milking was easy, but his hands got tired and many of the cows would not stand still. Tommy was having a better deal, he was naming the hens and finding the better layers. He was talking to them, and they seemed to be responding. Ally's pigs were aggressive, so Tommy started talking to them, they responded. Ally called Tommy the animal talker and watched in amazement when the animals responded.

Dora found some old clothes; her boys had worn when young and adjusted them to fit Ally and Tommy. One day Dora dressed them in their best clothes and made them stand outside the farmhouse. A lorry drove up and from the back a young man stumbled out. This was Elmer the son with one leg. Ally saw a soldier, so he saluted and Elmer saluted back. Elmer's mother and father rushed up to him and hugged him for the longest time. Finally he was introduced to Ally and Tommy. Frank begrudgingly said these two English had replaced Elmer and his brother. Elmer smiled and said they would surely do the job. Dora was smiling at her son.

After a few days Elmer appeared from his bedroom he had put on his wooden leg and wanted to walk around the garden. Ally and Tommy were very interested in his leg; they tried not to stare but were having sly looks at the leg. Elmer sat down took off his leg, threw it in the air and caught it. Ally and Tommy watched open mouthed.

"My lower leg was blown off by a mortar shell. I spent many months in England, and they made me this leg, any questions?"

"Do you have any feelings in the toes?"

"The obvious answer is of course no, but in fact I do sense some feelings in this leg. I often want to scratch the leg although I know it is wood. I have come to treat this piece of wood as though it was part of me, and I am sorry I cannot loan it to you two."

They all laughed at that remark. Now the boys and Elmer were friendly enough, so they complained about his father. This was a problem for Elmer. He knew his father was angry about having only half a son and wanting the farm to prosper. His two strong sons had been replaced by two young boys. These boys would grow to be big and strong, but the trick was to not drive them away. One night Elmer sat down with his father and had a frank talk.

"Father, you have lost a son and only have half a son. I have lost a brother and only have half of me. These two boys have lost both parents they have both lost two each. Leave them to me I will see they do their chores, but I will see they have some fun."

The boys were sitting with Dora in the kitchen and heard everything. Dora was smiling, her son was taking over. In future Frank relaxed and talked to the boys in a quiet voice.

Fall was spectacular with the colours of the tree leaves changing all the time. Tommy seemed to appreciate the scenery more than Ally but even he was impressed. They had chores all over the farm and could see the changes as winter approached. As winter was coming Elmer found some old ice skates in the basement. One pair was perfect for Ally but there was no pair that properly fit Tommy. Ally was a natural on skates and after few falls, he was away. Elmer was excited, he was showing Ally how to stop and to swerve and Ally was enjoying himself. Elmer started to tell Ally about ice hockey, this was the big winter sport in the region. It was always the English against the French.

Tommy was a problem he could not take to ice skating, and he only liked to kick a ball. Elmer gave him a ball like a rugby ball and said kick that. After a few attempts Tommy got the hang of kicking this ball. Elmer went to talk to his mother and said these two boys could do better than he or his brother. Ally was a natural on skates and Tommy understood how to kick a football. The vicar in his one room school was finding these two boys were his best pupils. Ally was always trying to answer questions but if he got the answer wrong Tommy invariably got it right. The vicar's only problem was that they were not too interested in religion; they blamed God for their parent's deaths.

Both Ally and Tommy were growing, and Dora was often modifying their clothing. They were also eating more, and Dora delighted in making large meals. She was thinking this pair ate more than her boys at a similar age. Frank was starting to appreciate having two strong lads about the farm. He was taking a back seat watching his son handle these growing boys. They were both growing strong fixing fences and digging garden plots. At the ice rink Ally had a few collisions with French boys but he could hold his own. Tommy was also growing strong, and boy could he kick that ball! Ally was catching and throwing the ball. Elmer was so pleased he asked the vicar if they could form a team of English boys to play Canadian Football. They contacted other Anglican schools and formed a team. Elmer would get the horse and trap taking Ally and Tommy to the practice field. A farmer would pick up the other boys with a horse and cart. Ally was the only one with a decent throwing arm and no one could kick like Tommy. He had been practicing place kicks, punts and his favourite the drop kick.

At school they had to learn French and some words in the local Quebecoise speech were different. They had a young French Canadian called Edouard to give them oral lessons. He recognized Ally and Tommy were very bright. Ally told him he was keen to play ice hockey and Tommy was enthusing about football. They invited him to watch them at a practice where he met Elmer. They knew each other from before Elmer went in the army. Edouard was impressed with Tommy's kicking and when he did a dropkick he was astounded.

"I have never seen a boy as young as him do a drop kick. There may not be many chances in a game but that was impressive, congratulations Tommy"

"Yes, I get great satisfaction out of doing those."

Edouard promised to get them a game with a team of similar ages. Elmer was trying to get the boys to play as a team but without a game he could not judge how they would go. Ally was the quarterback and Tommy was the wide receiver, punter and goal kicker. Most of the other boys had watched the game but never played it. One Saturday afternoon they had their first game, the clergy did not want them to play on a Sunday. The other team kicked off and Ally caught the ball. He was the biggest on his team and ran the ball back to the halfway line. This field was smaller than the conventional field due to the size of the players. Elmer instructed Ally to throw the ball to Tommy and if he caught it properly to drop it on to his foot and kick it forward and chase the ball. This would surely catch the opposing team off guard. The maneouver worked perfectly, and Tommy was tackled without the ball, a penalty which Tommy scored from the place kick.

The team was jubilant, but they had to kick off from the thirty-yard line (normally it would be the thirty five). Elmer told Tommy not to kick too hard but over the top of the receiver if he could. The receiver watched the ball sail over his head and there was an almighty scramble for the ball. That was the last chance Ally's team had to score until the second half. The other team played as a team and piled on the points. Ally became frustrated as the opposing team was giving Tommy a rough time. Elmer was continually telling Ally to calm down, it was all part of the game. Tommy said if he got a chance, he would try a field goal. Ally ran the ball a couple of times and made first downs (having to make ten yards in three tries). Tommy thought he could make a field goal, so he stood behind Ally and slotted home a perfect field goal. The umpire came and congratulated Tommy this was unheard of for boys of his age.

Their first game was a big loss but towards the end of the game they were starting to act as a team. Edouard had his team lined up and shake hands particularly with Ally and Tommy. They played several games that season and did not win a game, but they were getting better. Fall was approaching and both Ally and Tommy loved this season with the colours of the leaves in the variety of trees. They would walk for hours admiring the tree colours and Ally started to appreciate nature.

Ally talked to Edouard about getting a game of ice hockey, most of his football mates were too small for the rough and tumble of ice hockey. Edouard watched him skate and realized if he could handle the stick, he was going to be good. Ally was invited to a practice with some French-Canadian boys and a couple of Native Canadians. He was too fast for most of them, and they tried to push him against the boards, but he was too strong and could keep them at bay. Edouard had to step in a few times when things got heated. Elmer and Tommy watched with delight; Elmer was particularly excited at the way Ally handled himself.

On the farm both boys were doing a lot of the heavy lifting and were becoming strong. They were being noticed by some of the local girls. Even Elmer had his admirers and a few dances at the local village halls were a pleasure. Tommy was not yet ready for a girlfriend, but he encouraged Ally. Dora gave them the talk about the birds and bees and had Tommy and Ally both blushing. Elmer said his mother was a bit conservative, but she was talking sense.

"Tommy and I regard Dora as our mother and know she would not tell us anything wrong. The way she treats us we could not have a better mother; your mother is our mother. We understand she is more religious than us, but we respect her for that."

Now Elmer was blushing, the compliments were well deserved, these boys were his brothers not by blood but by sharing his mother. Even Frank was being called father.

Towards the end of the hockey season a man from Montreal came to watch a game. He told Elmer he wanted to sign Ally to a contract with a semi-professional team. As Ally was underage, he had to get his parents' signature. They would not use him until he was of age but wanted to retain him so that no other team would poach him. Elmer told him of the situation, but his parents were Ally's guardians. When Ally was told he said there was no problem as Frank and Dora were his stepparents.

The next two years were full of fun and work. The farm was doing well with milk and egg production much higher than previously. The garden plots were also producing well, and Dora was pickling both vegetables and fruit. Edouard's elder sister had taken an interest in Elmer, and she would come over and they would converse in Quebecois. The boys loved her, she was so friendly and knowledgeable. Tommy put it into words.

"Elmer, you should marry Claudette otherwise one of us will."

"You guys have a way of saying things I would not tolerate from others. There are plenty of obstacles to me marrying Claudette."

"They are all man-made obstacles, she is not German and only has two eyes, one head and ten toes. She is not a beauty queen but we recon she would make a fantastic wife and that is what you deserve. Do you mind if we discuss it with our mother."

"Yes, I do mind I need to have that discussion."

Ally and Tommy had forced Elmer's hand and they were very pleased with themselves. They had wanted to bring the subject out in the open; they were becoming a crafty pair. With the ice hockey and football they were making friends with the local French-Canadian boys (and girls). Neither of them was religious although they believed in heaven. They both freely talked to the vicar, who was their school master and the local parish priest. They actually liked the priest who told them stories about Quebec and was an ice hockey fanatic.

Elmer had talked to his mother and father and wanted a family meeting to discuss his possible wedding. This was unusual but Elmer was an unusual fellow and this was an unusual family. Dora liked Claudette but she was catholic. Frank could see problems with very different families. His family had fought for the farm and their problem was always the French. Ally was saying that two people in love should be together. Tommy took a different tack; he asked what was best for Elmer and would his marriage to Claudette split the family and would Claudette have more problems with her family than this one.

Elmer listened to all the arguments and said he would propose to Claudette, and she might turn him down. Ally said if she did, he would propose. Now they were all laughing. The mood was lightened, and they all had a drink of Frank's home brew including Dora. Claudette agreed to marry Elmer and said she would talk her family around. Many of them thought she was becoming an old maid. Edouard told the boys he was very pleased they had broken a taboo and he thought Elmer would make a perfect brother-in-law. Ally reminded him he would have two more brothers in law. Edouard laughed and said two extra brothers was no problem.

The next summer came and the man from Montreal appeared to watch the football games. He signed up Tommy as a kicker for another semi-professional team. Tommy was kicking the football unheard of distances for his age, and he had perfected the drop kick and could do it from the half way line. Frank was going to all the games and mixing with all the other parents, most of them farmers. He admitted that he knew more local people through these two boys; he was giving and sharing advice with other farmers. Elmer was preparing to get married, and Ally was going to be best man. Tommy would be a groom's man and guide people to their pews in the church. He had spied a couple of girls he wanted to guide to their places.

The church was full when Claudette entered on her father's arm, it was the Catholic Church. Elmer's relatives had never been in this church and found it very beautiful. The service was a shortened service with no reference to the Pope or Rome. The reception was in the church hall with plenty of food and drinks. There was a French-Canadian band that could play lots of English tunes. As best man Ally decided to give a long speech in Quebecois which included the war and

Canadian soldiers serving in Europe. He talked about his escape to Canada and finding a new family. He was a new Quebecker and he had to learn Quebecois and Elmer was his new brother. Edouard and Claudette were his teachers and so a brother and a teacher were a perfect match. His speech received a standing ovation and then it was over to the dancing.

Dora was hugging and kissing Ally, he had smoothed over the obstacles and now two different families were united. Elmer told him he now had a lady to scratch his wooden leg. Tommy was enjoying himself dancing with all the young ladies. Claudette came over and gave Ally a sly kiss and thanked him. Frank was enjoying some good French Brandy. It was all farm talk and of course about the newly married couple.

Ally joined a youth team in Montreal and would spend three days a week in Montreal, but he was always keen to get back to his chores on the farm. Elmer was coming up to his first wedding anniversary and Claudette was pregnant. Ally was being sponsored by a Montreal brewery and talked them into providing beer for the celebration. He told them it was good publicity and they agreed. A celebration with free beer could not fail to be a hit. Both families were now familiar with each other and so they all enjoyed the party. All the young cousins were good friends and Tommy was the French families' favourite.

Tommy was growing stronger and captaining the football team and they started to win games. He teased Ally that they could win without him. Both Elmer and Claudette were coaching the football team and Claudette had recruited a couple of French boys who made all the difference. When Tommy received the ball in the back field the other team was not sure whether he would throw punt or try a field goal. Claudette was saying she wanted a boy, but Elmer was saying there was a shortage of girls in his family. Even though Claudette was in her last weeks of pregnancy she would not miss a game.

Claudette had a girl and both families were celebrating. Ally and Tommy were not used to newborn babies; she was so small. They were afraid to hold her, they were used to newborn pigs and calves but this was different. Elmer was in a very happy mood even telling Edouard he should get married. Edouard said he was not ready yet, so Ally told him to come to Montreal he had seen some hot ladies. These four were just like brothers. Ally found that Edouard's younger brothers were not so friendly; they were not unfriendly.

While Ally was in Montreal he started to think of his real family. He pulled out the wedding photo, the ten-shilling note and his little black diary. That diary had him thinking about his parents and he decided to approach the British consulate to get birth certificates and a marriage certificate. The consulate had a record of Ally coming to Canada and his birth certificate was easy. Once he had his parent's full names and their birthdays from his little black diary it was easy to get the other documents. Ally was praising the policeman who gave him the diary. His parent's birth certificates gave the names of his grandparents and he vowed to look them up if ever he was able to get to Britain. He knew his surname was McGregor, but he did not know his mother's maiden name was Sinclair.

After playing a couple of seasons in Montreal the brewery was talked into sponsoring an exhibition tour of Britain. Ally got in the ear of the senior managers and told them they should visit London, Birmingham, Manchester, Glasgow and Edinburgh. He said London and Edinburgh were a must and the other cities were big beer drinking cities. One of the board members said that Ally should be recruited as an advertising manager as he had so many good ideas. Ally had picked London and Edinburgh as his grandparents lived near those capitals. He had also arranged a few days in each city so the team could relax. The team coach was astonished at how Ally had arranged everything. Ally had also told the brewery that they could use him as an advert. He was originally English and now he was skating as good as any Canadian. The brewery hierarchy was very impressed

Tommy was happy for Ally as he left for Britain. His only comment was to visit where they lived in Birmingham. Ally had planned that, and he was going to visit a police station. The flight to London was long but whereas his teammates were half asleep he was wide awake. The next day he left the team to find his grandparents. He had to look up the exact address in the telephone directory. As he approached the front door of the address, he had he felt a sudden uncertain feeling. It manifested itself as a sweat and an increased heartbeat. He knocked the door, and an elderly lady came to the door. She was a bit wary of this well-built young man standing before her.

"Do not be alarmed, are you Mrs Sinclair?"

"Yes."

"Then I am your grandson and I have a wedding photo as proof."

Ally had already seen the resemblance to his mother. On seeing the photo Mrs Sinclair burst into tears. She invited him into the house and excused herself as she had to call her husband to come home as soon as possible. Ally told his story after his grandmother had composed herself. His grandfather arrived before his grandmother had gotten far into her story. Ally's mother had strict parents and at eighteen had left home. They did not know where she had gone and knew nothing of Ally. There was always of the belief his mother would come back home. With such chaos after the war they could not find her. Her death was the last thing that occurred to them. His grandfather was a merchant banker, and they were wealthy; they wanted Ally to live with them. Ally explained he had a family in Canada, and he had to find his father's family. He invited them to come watch him play ice hockey. His grandmother did not want him to leave but his grandfather realized Ally was his mother's son. Two extra spectators watched the game, and they were so proud of their grandson. He had plenty of hugs after the game. Two wills were suddenly changed especially after Ally told them his mother had kissed him goodbye after giving him breakfast. Both grandparents could not stop crying after hearing that.

In Birmingham Ally recognized the ice rink. He was able to look for his home and found there were new houses on the site. Tommy's site was still empty. He could not find his favourite policeman at the station on Dudley Road, but he invited the policemen to come see an ice hockey match; several of them came.

The local newspapers had heard that Ally was from Birmingham and so he was interviewed. These reporters had never heard about Quebecois and so he gave them a quick lesson. They also knew almost nothing about ice hockey and so another lesson. Luckily one reporter from a small newspaper knew about ice hockey and he told Ally he would follow them to Manchester and Glasgow. Ally invited him to Shawinigan if he ever got that way. He then had to explain the location of Shawinigan.

In Edinburgh he found a local who could take him to the address he had for his grandparent. This was huge estate and Ally was hoping he had the correct address. He was greeted at the door by a butler and Ally asked to see Mr McGregor.

"You mean the laird, who may I ask is visiting his worship?"

"I am his grandson Alistair McGregor." "Please wait here sir I will talk to him."

Ally was standing on the steps of a huge house and looking around at well-kept fields. This estate was so large he started to wonder how many cattle they had. An elderly gentleman with a short white beard came to the door.

"You must be my father's and uncle Jock's father but as proof they are both on this photo." As the laird looked at the photo he had tears in his eyes, he called to the butler to call his wife. He then realized they were standing on the steps and invited Ally inside the house. Suddenly Ally's grandfather hugged Ally with such force Ally struggled to breath. His grandmother was crying before she kissed him. When Ally told them that when he first met his uncle he could not understand what he said, his grandmother was both laughing and crying at the same time. He told them that as a McGregor his uncle had told him to look after his mates and he had always followed that creed. Uncle Jock had promised to get him when the war was over but for several years Ally did not know he was dead. He had visions of his uncle playing bagpipes on the D Day beach. Now both his grandparents were crying.

His grandfather told him the story. Ally's father was the eldest son and had an argument with his father and had left home. They had no idea where he went, and they did not know he was married and had a son. Jock had known but he was sworn to secrecy and his secret died on D Day. Ally's grandmother could not stop staring at the wedding photo and asked if they could get a copy. Ally said they must return the original as it was one of his three prized possessions. He invited them to see him play and told them his family in Canada were awaiting his return. A group of McGregor's came to watch him play and he had a cheer squad. After the game Ally met the extended family and they were all asking him to stay in Scotland. Ally said he had a family and a life in Canada but would visit one day. His grandmother told him he was Jo's son, and she was proud of him.

Ally returned to Canada after a side trip to Paris where they played another exhibition match. His teammates thought that they would be understood in Paris but Ally's English and French was more acceptable than their Quebecois. The brewery was very happy they had two new investors who had bought a lot of their stock. The two investors were called Sinclair and McGregor and they had a license to sell their product in England and Scotland.

Ally met his new family and told them about his trip to Britain and his new relatives. Tommy listened intently.

"Tommy you should go to England and trace your relatives."

"No thank you, they have never looked for me so why should I look for them. I have a great family here and I want no other. Quebec and Canada are my home, and I would not live anywhere else."

Lots of travel ending in Canada

Trevor was born at the beginning of the war (WWII), his father had served in the army and was now in the home guard. His father had been a sergeant in the army but had been invalided out of the army. Trevor never knew the reason until much later. Near the end of the war Trevor started infant school. He loved school and made lots of friends. Most of his friends had been in the same street but now he met other kids from the same area. At the end of the infants he was transferred to a junior school. This school was a catholic school and he had to make new friends; that was no problem for Trevor. Most of his old friends went to a different school but he still played with them in the street or in the park.

This was a time of new freedoms; the end of rationing and he could buy sweets. He could buy but rarely could afford. Most of his friends would share their bounty but none of them had much to share; this was a relatively poor area. Most of the games involved boys and girls, at nine or ten years old the girls were as good and as strong as the boys. Even playing football, some of the girls were better than the boys.

He was about eleven preparing to go to senior school and the boys and girls still were playing in the street. One Saturday afternoon Trevor was approached by one of the fathers.

"You're a catholic, you cannot play with my daughters."

The man then took his daughters home. The rest of the boys and girls stood silently watching and not understanding this development. When Trevor told his mom she said he should ignore that man. That night he heard his mom and dad arguing, they argued occasionally so Trevor ignored it. He thought he heard something about religion, but he was sleepy and not interested. When he went into senior school, he noticed his parents were often arguing. After his twelfth birthday his mother had a fight with his father, and she left for Ireland. His father told Trevor his mother would come back when she cooled down, but she never did return. Trevor found that his father would spend more time in the pub and Trevor would have to look after himself.

Trevor left school at fifteen and found a job at Scribanns bakery helping deliver bread. He was on a horse drawn cart with an older delivery man. Jo his boss was a happy fellow who had the horse trained so he almost never had to take control of the cart. The horse knew the whole route and Jo knew all the customers and all their orders. Trevor loved this horse it was so obedient and seemed to love being brushed.

There was plenty of time to chat. One day Trevor said, "I am a Catholic. Do you mind?"

Jo laughed and said, "Maybe you should mind *me*; I am an atheist. I don't believe in God."

"I thought everyone believed in God."

"Most do but not me but I am not going to try to convert you and you have no chance of converting me. Religion and politics are the curse of every society."

That gave Trevor a lot of food for thought. He asked his father whether he believed in God.

"Sometimes but not always, I think you are growing up and I am glad you need to think for yourself."

Trevor was enjoying his time with Jo, but he was becoming restless he wanted to try something new. Actually there were plenty of jobs available, but he thought he would like to travel. He only knew a small part of Birmingham and had never been to other parts of England. One night he sat down with his father to discuss the future.

"I am so happy I have a seventeen-year-old thinking about the future. I am not sure whether I had similar thoughts at your age. You could join the army as you will probably be conscripted when you are eighteen. The army could give you plenty of opportunities to travel but no choice. Joining early will give you a head start on the others who are conscripted. You will probably have to sign up for four or five years but by then you will have seen a bit of life and can make a reasonable choice of what you want to do. I have never told you this but for many years I enjoyed the army, but something happened. I was told it was like a mental breakdown. I suddenly became very violent, sometimes when I had a drink but not every time. They locked me up for a while and then invalided me out of the army. The doctors could not diagnose what was wrong with me, but they gave me tablets that would calm me when I got agitated.

I never hurt your mother, but she became afraid of me and left to go back to her family. I could never fathom why she left you with me but in some ways, you became a calming influence. I have had a few punch ups down the pub, but I am learning to control myself. The knowledge of having to look after you had a desired effect."

Trevor listened in silence and vowed to join the army. He now knew why his father had left the army. In 1957 Trevor joined the army before being conscripted. He did his basic training at Aldershot, lots of marching and keeping his clothes clean and tidy, something new to him. The word in his troop was that they were to be sent to Germany. Instead they were sent to Cypress. He had to look up Cypress on the map; he had no idea where it was. His sergeant told him they were going to keep the Greeks and Turks apart. Now Trevor was busy in the library trying to find out as much as he could about Cypress. His mates were only glad to leave Aldershot.

Arriving in Cypress he thought they had sent him to a seaside resort. They were sent to a camp where one perimeter was a beach. After one night's sleep the troop were issued with batons and shields and then sent to a village. They had no guns, only the officers had guns. In the middle of the village was a barrier and they were two group either side of the barrier. The sergeant explained that the Turkish Cypriots would approach from one side and the Greek Cypriots form the other side. They were there to keep them apart. Trevor was thinking *how do we escape* and how could he tell the difference between a Greek and a Turk? These were peaceful demonstrations but if the opposing side met it could become violent. All he had to do was swing his baton and keep the two forces at bay. His shield was to be used to fend off projectiles such as rocks and stones.

After about fifteen minutes his arm was getting tired swinging his baton. He had not hit anyone, and he was hoping not to do so. Finally he was relieved by new troops and was able to relax. He then looked at the opposing forces and could not detect any difference. The only difference was the flags they were carrying. On the way back to camp they were greeted by many English people outside grandiose villas.

After the first week he found a captain and asked him what these constant demonstrations were about.

"You are the first soldier to ask me that question. The Greeks are mainly Orthodox Christians, and the

Turks are mainly Moslems. Some Greeks want to unite with Greece. The Turks think they will be disenfranchised."

"What is disenfranchised?"

"It means loss of rights or privilege's, such as voting rights."

"Ah religion and politics, I used to have lots of discussions with my old boss, he was an atheist. He told me religion and politics were the scourge of the world and here I am seeing an example."

"Yes, there is another side consisting of some Greeks, Turks, rich Europeans and British who want us to stay. Their reason is economic they feel that their investments might disappear if Greece takes over."

"Yes money, religion and politics they are a good combination for strife. I have seen the lovely villas and the occupants and now I know why they seem glad we are here."

Trevor started to take an interest in politics, and he was able to get an English language newspaper printed on the island. He was learning about enosis and starting to understand this beautiful island. Within a couple of weeks he was promoted to Lance Corporal, and he thought it must be the captain's doing.

The demonstrations seemed to be getting fewer, so it was decided his squad was needed elsewhere. Now lance corporal Trevor in 1959 was off to Kenya to combat the Mau Mau. Arriving in Kenya they found they were only used to guard the internment camps.

Just pockets of Mau Mau remained but the conditions in the camps were very poor, and Trevor had to bite his tongue quite often. He talked to one of the officers (he seemed to have a knack of approaching officers) and found as his squad were used to crowd control they were going to be shipped to Aden. Trevor had no control about his world travels but was glad to get out of Kenya. The officer explained that Aden was not an easy posting. The locals wanted to get rid of the British and their demonstrations were more violent than those in Cypress. His troop would try to keep the peace with batons and shields, but they would also carry rifles and may have cause to use them.

The climate in Aden was hot and humid but they would still be dressed in full uniform except they might be allowed to wear shorts. In Kenya the camps were near Nairobi and the weather pleasant. The climate in Aden was energy sapping.

The officer was correct, being posted to Aden was a different kettle of fish to Cypress. Swinging a baton was more tiring than in Cypress. They carried a water bottle but that was soon finished. Besides full uniform they carried a rifle and the officers carried pistols. Their shields were in constant use as all manner of missiles were thrown at them. One minor compensation for Trevor was that he was promoted to corporal. Trevor's squad was a closely knit bunch and they soon found that having a hangover (beer in the mess) made life almost impossible the next day.

Trevor liked a beer but was able to convince his men to have only two beers and drink plenty of water.

Only once did his whole squad need to use their guns. They were about to replace another troop when an officer lined them up and told them to fire in the air. The fire was rather sporadic, and Trevor suggested his men needed some practice on the firing range. This was probably the reason he was promoted to sergeant. He and two of his men were instructed how to fire tear gas canisters. These were useful when the demonstrators became violent, but they had to be aware of the wind direction. Trevor's mates used tear gas a couple of times to good effect. A few of his men were injured by flying missiles but they did not have to shoot anyone although the snipers from his squad used plenty of ammunition. Trevor was never able to understand this conflict. He could not read the local newspapers and many of the officers could not give him a clear explanation. He often wondered what the British were doing in Aden.

His squad was now all regular soldiers. His last conscripts had gone home, and he was glad to have a permanent bunch of men as comings and goings were not good for discipline. He never really had a problem with discipline as he always discussed every situation with his men. The only problem was they kept asking him how long before they left this hell hole. All he could do was to suggest to the officers that his men needed a bit of a rest. It must have had an effect as they were now posted to Singapore.

One officer explained that Singapore was similar to Aden, climate wise, but much more civilized (the officer's observation). Trevor's squad was picked up by a destroyer and as they left the dock Trevor told them not to cheer too loudly as there were many poor buggers left in Aden. His squad loved his sense of humour. For some reason the sailors were not too friendly, but his troop entertained themselves. Trevor allowed them to have more than two beers but warned them inspection and drill would be better without a hangover.

They landed in Singapore and were transported to the garrison. The barracks in Singapore were very comfortable and the fans much appreciated. There were a few drills in the morning but in the afternoon, there were a few lectures. Most of the lectures were boring but Trevor encouraged his men to be seen at the lectures even if they hated them. Later in the day Trevor loved to walk around the local markets and get to understand the various nationalities that lived in this city. He always wore his uniform and in general he was greeted with smiles and polite words. Actually he was more interested in the people who frowned at him and often told him to go home. He always tried to get them into conversation to get to know why he should go home. One man told him that he should go to the rich areas and see how they lived. Trevor took that as good advice.

Trevor decided to walk around the richer areas where there were hotels and even a cricket pitch. The houses were almost like palaces and generally had guards at the front gates. Many of these guards were Sikhs and Trevor often stopped and entered into conversations with them. He liked these men they were often ex-soldiers. In other areas there were many stalls where he could get cold drinks but this day he was in area where there appeared to be no street sellers, so he went to a hotel. At the entrance he was told "sorry soldier officers only," it was the same at the next hotel. Trevor had never been turned away from any establishment and he was angry. Suddenly he was looking at Aden in a new light.

Trevor did not tell his troops his opinion and bottled up his anger. His troops were enjoying a well-earned rest and he appreciated that. He now started to buy local newspapers to try and understand local politics. At one of the lectures he asked a few questions about Malaya and the politics of the people. The lecturer did not answer his questions either through ignorance or because it was a delicate subject. In the market he found that laughter was the way to mix and although he never bought much many of the stall holders became friendly. He even went to a wedding where he watched Singaporeans enjoying themselves. Luckily, they had alcoholic drinks and he sampled some good local beer. He was also told that if he was sent to northern Malaya, he should be very careful as the communists were out to kill British. Trevor thought nothing of it until after a couple of days he found he was going to take a train ride to the north.

Now Trevor started to think how his friends had known of his imminent journey and more importantly who else knew. They were going by train and his troop would occupy the front two carriages behind the engine. As they boarded the train they did so with unloaded rifles. Once the officers had gone back to their carriages at the back of the train Trevor told his troops to load their guns. Trevor had consulted maps, but he had no idea where they could have trouble. Trevor had a bad feeling about this trip and so he took a tour of the two front carriages. The front carriage had a platform between the back of the tender and the coal was stacked up before the driver and the crew. His mates were enjoying their train ride, but Trevor was thinking of how you would attack a train. Some of the old cowboy films he had seen at the Grove cinema came back to mind.

He was enjoying his childhood memories when the train started to break heavily. He shouted, "Get down!" and rushed to the second carriage with the same order. Suddenly gun fire smashed through the windows luckily most of the men were under the tables and only one got hit by flying glass. Now Trevor breathed deeply and took command.

"Keep down, poke your rifles over the windowsill and fire into the bush. I want alternate fire: one man fires, and then the next man fires while the first reloads. I don't care if you hit anything or not, just keep firing."

The men who are near the divides between the windows were told to look at what they could see but not to poke their heads past their protection. Three men were ordered to fix bayonets in case "someone wants to join us." This rapid fire went for about five minutes, they had plenty of ammunition. Trevor told them to stop and listen if there was any return fire. Actually after the first burst of fire that had broken the widows there had been little return fire.

Suddenly there was knock on the front door of the carriage.

"Cover me, I will open the door but do not fire unless he points a gun. I think anyone who knocks wants to come in."

Trevor opened the door and one of the firemen came in with his hands up. Now the troop burst into laughter, anyone who knocks must want to come in had seemed so funny to them. The man explained that the driver and his mate had been killed but he had hidden in the coal.

Suddenly there was a knock at the second carriage door, the soldiers shouted enter and trained their rifles at the door; in walked an officer. One wag shouted our sergeant said we should shoot any armed man who came through that door. Luckily the officer saw the funny side of the joke.

Now Trevor asked for a volunteer to climb on to the roof of the carriage to see whether any of their assailants were still in place. There was silence.

"Okay I will go but if I don't come back, it has been good to know you all."

"No sarge you are too valuable; I am the smallest and present the smallest target."

This was 'little' Charley named because he was the smallest in the troop.

"Don't get killed or I will blame myself."

"Don't worry sarge, if I get killed, I will blame you as well."

The whole troop started to laugh and even the officer saw the funny side. Charley moved slowly outside followed by Trevor. This carriage had a ladder to the roof, so Charley had no problem getting in position. Trevor was watching for any movement in the bushes, he was hoping for none and there was none. Charley shouted that there was no movement but there appeared to be a body at the end of the bush. It did not look alive, but he could not be sure. Most of the attack seemed to come from the left side of the train but Charley said he could see nothing on the right side.

Trevor sent two men to the engine on the right side of the train and instructed them that if it was clear he would send the fireman. He was worried the engine might be building up too much steam pressure. Now he decided to investigate the body in the bush on the left side. He had several men covering him, he had picked the better shots as he did not want to be shot by his own men. Trevor approached the body with caution, but he thought he saw a second body. He lay flat for a while trying to get a better view of the second body. These were poorly clothed peasants, and he could not see their arms. He realized the rifle of a dead man would have been removed by his mates. The first man had been shot in the neck and had bled to death. The second man had been shot twice, once in the chest and once in the head. Trevor thought that he had been killed by his friends as they could not move him. This was later confirmed by an army doctor on the train. The bullet in the head was of a caliber not used by the British army.

Now it seemed that all the train passengers were out looking at the macabre scene. Trevor called all his men back into the train and told Charley to come back. He told them to let the souvenir hunters get shot if any dissidents were still present. Trevor was in a bad mood, why were all his soldiers in the front carriages? The rear carriages were untouched and maybe some people in Singapore knew the attack would occur. Later he had his men clear the barrier that had made the train stop.

Up country Malaya was very different from Singapore. The area where they were stationed was like a large rubber plantation. Everything was orderly with good roads and plenty of traffic taking rubber to the port or refineries. This state of Johor was very rich and there were plenty of Clubs with tennis courts, fields for football and cricket. Trevor had jeep transport and was welcomed into the clubs (very different from Singapore). His troop was stationed with Malayan troops, and they were very friendly. Trevor thought he could live here; he loved the countryside. Unfortunately they only stayed a few months and were summoned back to Singapore. Trevor was not keen to leave but this was the army.

In Singapore he started to mix with the students who supported Lee Quan Yew who was to become prime minister in 1965. Trevor was interested in politics and wanted to know more about a multicultural society. The student organizations were mainly Chinese but there were also Indians and Malays. His interest in politics came to the notice of the Army Intelligence Unit. The army decided to move Trevor on to a new post. Trevor was warned he might be sent to Belize but that was changed to Hong Kong. Trevor had looked up Belize on the map and was quite looking forward to visiting the Americas.

This time Trevor had to leave his mates behind, he was going to replace a newly retired sergeant. There was more than one garrison in Hong Kong, and he was sent to the largest. He first went to Victoria barracks, where he had to sit with new arrivals given lectures on

Hong Kong. They visited all the garrisons and were taken to the border with China. There he met Gurkhas protecting the border. Trevor and his group went to all the port areas protected by the army and also were shown the market areas. Trevor was impressed with Victoria barrack it even had a swimming pool.

Trevor was to be based at Osborn barracks in Kowloon. The first thing he noticed was that Kowloon was more densely populated than Hong Kong Island. He could hardly fail to notice the density of the traffic. He was greeted by the garrison commander who invited him to his office. Trevor thought that was a good start.

"I see from your record you have been to more places than me. The army has certainly moved you around. I also see that you have been involved with crowd control and that could be useful. Also in your record is that have had plenty of interaction with Chinese in Singapore. Do you know any Cantonese?"

"Only a little bit sir but most of the Chinese students had excellent English, in many cases better English than me."

"Do you think you could learn Cantonese?"

"Yes, sir but I would have to mix with the local population."

"Well, our main task here in Kowloon is to guard the docks and help the police keep order in the markets. There is so much going on in this area and the information we get is often unreliable. Organized crime with gangs involved in smuggled goods is just one problem they also run the opium trade, prostitution and gambling. It is our duty to keep order, but the police rely on us a lot."

"Do you think I could take a course or two in a local college? I have always wanted to be an accountant when I left the army."

"Brilliant idea, these colleges will be full of Chinese."

The commandant was very impressed with Trevor and gave him as much free time as possible. Trevor decided he needed civilian clothes and so he found a tailor. These tailors were mainly Indian who spoke Hindi (not useful to Trevor) English and Cantonese. His visits to the tailors helped him learn some Cantonese as he was always asking questions. He was also very satisfied with his new clothes. The commandant was kept informed with what he was doing. The commander was impressed and realized he had found a gem.

In the market he would ask the names of fruit or vegetables but never get into conversation with the stall holders. He found a couple of policemen with whom he tried conversation as he thought they would not divulge his knowledge. The next problem was the Chinese characters. In the library he found a book that had some characters with English meaning. He noted that the book had rarely been borrowed. Trevor spent several hours copying these characters and then would get one of 'his' policemen and point to a sign and give its meaning. Sometimes he got it correct but it was more informative when he got it wrong. The policeman would write the correct script and Trevor would have the meaning of two scripts.

Trevor decided he had to investigate the night life. Several of the soldiers told him there were plenty of places to go dancing. He decided for his first dance he would go to a church hall. He went in one of his new suits. This dance did not have alcohol, but it did not worry Trevor as he was not a regular drinker. He sat at a table with a glass of lemonade and spied a beautiful Chinese girl. He approached her and in his best Cantonese asked for a dance. She looked at him and said, "I think my English is better than your Cantonese, but I will dance with you."

Trevor found out that this beautiful girl in a long black dress was called Li Lin. She also told him he had tried to translate English into Cantonese and had lost the meaning. This first dance was a pleasure on many fronts. A second dance taught him a bit more about dancing. Li Lin left early so he could not get a third dance, but she had told him she would be at the same dance next week.

Back in the barracks all he could think about was Li Lin. He had met a few girls in Singapore, but Li Lin was a level above them. She was slim and facially so good looking, she moved with ease and copped with his awful dancing. Her English was very good, and he had no problem talking to her. She had broken the ice by telling him about his Cantonese. He had to go back next week.

There were problems stirring in Hong Kong, a lot of it related to the cultural revolution in China. Trevor volunteered for a morning shift so he could have time in the evening. He was worried that the dance might be cancelled. It was not cancelled, and Trevor sat at the table with Li Lin. He met her sister Meng and tried a bit of Cantonese much to the delight of the sisters. They now gave him a lesson in Cantonese. He was not offended but loving his lesson. The dancing was better, and he danced with both sisters. Meng was obviously older and not as good looking as Li Lin, but he found it was easier to dance with her. He put it down to the feeling he was in love with Li Lin. During one of the dances with Li Lin, she told him she was not a prostitute, and she was only here to dance.

"I am not looking for a prostitute and I have also come to enjoy a dance."

He said that in English so as not to be misunderstood. They both laughed and enjoyed the dance. At the end of the evening he offered to escort the sisters' home, they both accepted. During the walk Li Lin asked Trevor what he did for a living, and he told her he was in the army.

"Why are you not in uniform?"

"This is my free time, and I don't dance in uniform I only march."

Over the next few weeks he learned that Li Lin and Meng had escaped the communist forces with their mother and come to Hong Kong. Their father had been killed by the communists and their mother had died not long after getting to Hong Kong. The two girls had found jobs in the sewing 'sweat' shops and saved enough money to buy their own sewing machine. Now Meng was in charge of one of the sweat shops and Li Lin was going alone with her machine. Trevor realized these girls had gumption. The real good thing about this relationship was that his Cantonese was improving leaps and bounds. His commander was informed about all these developments. At one of the dances, Li Lin said Trevor should not take them home as she was worried about his safety. She had heard that there would be demonstration very soon. Trevor smiled to himself on the walk to the barracks; Li Lin was more worried about his safety than the army.

There were demonstrations but they seemed to be more intense on Hong Kong Island and Kowloon was relatively quiet. Trevor thought the local traders and the gangs were more interested in business than politics. His police friends were telling him that the level of crime had decreased as they thought some of the bad guys had left Kowloon.

Trevor was seriously in love with Li Lin and talked to his commanding officer about getting permission to marry. He was now very friendly with his commander who told him to think seriously about interracial marriage. He also asked if Li Lin would marry him, and she should take a couple of weeks to think over the problem. Trevor was regularly kissing and fondling but Li Lin had bluntly told him she would not have intercourse before marriage. Good and bad news but she was obviously interested in marriage.

Trevor did not know many people in Hong Kong and did not know any interracial couples. He decided to talk to Li Lin about cultural problems possibly leading to marital problems. She outsmarted him and told him marriages between Europeans and Chinese were difficult because of interference from one or other family problems. She only had a sister and an uncle in Canada she hardly knew. He only had a father, as far as she knew, in England and fathers seemed to be less of a problem than mothers. Her sister liked Trevor and she would never be a problem. She had outsmarted him and come to the point straight away. She did not know he had a living mother, but he had never had contact with her, so she did not matter.

Trevor proposed and apologized for not having a ring prepared but his decision was a spur of the moment event. Li Lin was so happy and accepted straight away. She called Meng and they all kissed and hugged. As Trevor walked home to the barracks, he felt he was floating; the last hour had been just like a dream. Back in his room he composed two letters, one to his father and one to Charley. He was still in Singapore and had been promoted to corporal.

The wedding was a civil wedding and Meng had found a flat so Li Lin and Trevor could live in their place. The commandant was very happy for Trevor especially when he saw Li Lin and gave Trevor permission to live outside the garrison. Life with Li was just a pleasure, she would try to fulfil his every wish and he had plenty. She was an excellent lover, and he would often lie in bed next to his nude wife and stoke her tender skin. Actually he preferred her in that long black dress. They often went dancing with Meng and he would have pleasure dancing with them both. He talked to them about getting a second sewing machine and a place to work together.

"I love having you both together and I can keep the accounts. I think there is a possibility of doing good business."

Meng said she would help buy the sewing machine.

"Meng there is no need I have plenty of money and I want this family to prosper. We are a great family, and you are an essential part of it, and you can keep Li company when I am not around."

It was settled and the sewing business took off.

The sergeant major in the garrison was retiring and Trevor was promoted to sergeant major. One of his new responsibilities was to look after the mess. In fact there were three messes, one for the officers, one for the NCO's and one for the other soldiers. Besides his other duties he was in control of all the messes and kept the keys to the three tills and organized the opening, closing and cleaning of the mess. Most of the barmen and cleaners were Chinese but he had some soldiers controlling the stock and a couple of military police to keep order. Trevor also kept the accounts. The tills had a second set of keys kept by the commander; these were kept in a safe with a combination only known by the commander and Trevor.

Everything was going smoothly for six months; the sewing shop was earning good money and Trevor had a routine. Cleaners would come in the morning, and he would open the tills and clear them and put back the floats and bank the takings. He would then open the mess for lunchtime. He would close the mess in the afternoon for more cleaning (he hated the smell of stale spilt beer). In the evening he would open the mess, go home and come back near closing time when he would lock all the tills. In the morning he would count the till contents and bank the profits and record the takings. One Saturday morning he opened the tills, and they were all empty except for small change. Friday night was always busy, and he knew there would have been hundreds of pounds in the tills. He immediately reported to the commander. They opened the safe and found the other keys. Trevor always kept his set of keys in a small pocket in his tunic and they were always there.

The barmen were all questioned as were the soldiers who looked after the stock. Even the military police were questioned. Trevor showed the commander the books and the taking should have been several hundred pounds. Each till had a float of one hundred pounds. The commander said there would have to be a court of enquiry.

Now Trevor was facing a problem and he could not think how the tills had been opened. There was no evidence they had been forced. His evidence was that he was innocent and did not need the money. He had never done anything illegal in his life. The court had no option but to find him guilty and his service was terminated with a dishonourable discharge.

Trevor sat at home for several days in shock. Li tried to help him but after the initial shock came anger. He started to drink and then one night he started to think about his mother. She had left his father because she was afraid and now he was probably going down the same path. He apologized to Li and said he would try to find a job. The problem was that word of his dismissal was all over Hong Kong and no one would employ him. He wrote to Charley and gave every detail. He could not bring himself to write to his father. He met one of the officers who was in Osborn barracks, and he told him that having a Chinese wife had gone against him. This really upset Trevor and made him angry again. He decided he had to leave Hong Kong.

Charley's reply cheered him up a bit. Charley could never believe Trevor had stolen the money. He suggested a third set of keys or maybe someone who could pick locks. Trevor discounted that idea as he locked up on Friday night and on the Saturday as he let in the cleaners, he had gone to the tills, but he was glad someone was on his side.

Li could see her husband's frustration and suggested they go to England. Trevor thought she must be reading his mind. Li told him Meng could take care of the workshop and if England did not work out, they could come back to Hong Kong. Now Trevor had a trip to plan and that put his problems in the back of his mind. He warned his father that he had left the army and would bring his wife to Birmingham. He also contacted Charley and asked if they could visit Singapore. Charley's reply was very welcoming.

Trevor had always travelled free with the army; this was the first time he had to pay his own way. As a paying guest with no responsibilities he thought he could enjoy a long voyage especially with his beautiful wife. They could get a ship to Singapore and then later another ship to England. Li noticed the change in her husband as he was planning the trip. Trevor saved plenty of money from his service and the court had not asked for compensation probably because they had no evidence of his theft.

At the docks Meng and Li were in tears and Trevor was close to it; he promised they would be back. As they sailed out of the harbour Li was telling him she had never seen these sights. Then she asked Trevor what they had to do and all he could say was enjoy themselves. He did warn her that the food could be different, and he was not sure they would have much Chinese food. Li was not fazed by the food, but the service was more than she expected.

The bedroom pleasure in the cabin was good except they had bad weather for a couple of days when she just hung on to Trevor, much to his delight. They had a cabin with a porthole and Li spent a lot of time at that porthole. Up on deck she was perturbed with no sight of land, she could not swim.

Arriving in Singapore they were greeted by Charley and his wife Nur. They all greeted each other and then Nur decided to practice her Cantonese. Li was in tears as she answered, and Trevor translated for Charley. Charley apologized as he only spoke English except for a few unacceptable phrases in a few languages. Everyone laughed and Li hugged Nur.

The next two weeks were a pleasure for Li, Nur took her everywhere in Singapore and Charley and Trevor visited a few hotels where Trevor had been denied entry. Charley's father-in-law owned a block of flats. Trevor and Li stayed in a top floor flat, and Li could not get over the view. Li and Nur talked about everything and became good friends. Charley and Trevor talked about the army and families. Charley liked his in-laws, and they liked him, he had to ban one of Nur's cousins as he always wanted money, he was a gambler. Charley's mother was against the marriage, he had married a brown girl. He had more or less cut her off. Trevor explained that his sister-in-law Meng was a woman he wished was his real sister.

Inevitably the subjects came around to politics. Charley was very happy with Lee Quan Yew; he was running a very tight ship and Singapore was progressing. They also discussed Cypress and Aden; Kenya was not their favourite place. Trevor was worried what he could do in England and also how his father and Li would get on. Charley was comforting by saying what he could see of Li she would adapt to any situation, but he warned Trevor she would need some warm clothing. Clothing had escaped Trevor's plans but luckily, he found a store which specialized in clothes for Singaporeans travelling to Europe.

Li was surprised and amused at these clothes especially stockings and cardigans. Trevor explained that even in summer she might feel cold. He bought a coat, slacks and comfortable shoes. He was cursing he had planned their trip but never had a thought about clothing. Even some of his clothing was probably too light for England. He had left his uniform in Hong Kong.

Leaving Singapore was a repeat of leaving Hong Kong. Nur was begging Li to come back, and Charley was saying they would be welcome anytime. Trevor was very happy what he had seen in Singapore. He had refrained from contacting some of his old friends. Trevor understood that many had positions in the government. He was very pleased to visit hotels that had denied him previously, for him that was a triumph.

The voyage to England was interesting. Of course they avoided Aden but going through the Suez Canal had them both enthralled, Li was as much interested in the desert as in the canal. Visiting Gibraltar was a delight as they were able to get a city tour, Li enjoyed the organization she had never been on a city tour before, and the guide was telling them the sights. As they came into the English Channel Li was appreciating her warm clothing. Landing in Southampton was fascinating for Li, everything was so organized. She loved the train journey to Birmingham. The train was so clean and the scenery so organized, but Birmingham station had her in awe. It was the biggest building she had ever been inside.

They arrived in a taxi at Trevor's home to be greeted by his father. There was a bit of hesitancy in the greeting, but Li hugged her father-in-law and that broke the ice. As Trevor expected the house was a bit of a mess and he and Li started to tidy the place. Trevor's father John was not too happy, but he watched them clean up the place. He told them to settle in as he was going to the pub. Trevor was not too happy, but Li told him to let his father live his own life.

The next day Trevor told his father about the theft and his discharge. His father was not too sympathetic and that hurt Trevor. Li calmed him and said that his father did not know the whole story. In the next few weeks Trevor was trying to find a job but his military service was always brought up and so no job. He could have a job as security on the markets, but he wanted an accountant job. Li had found a job in a Chinese restaurant and was actually enjoying her interaction with Chinese and English employees. The customers were not always a pleasure.

Trevor decided they should have a weekend in London. He had never been to London and had little ideas what to see. Li had learned about the Kings Road and Carnaby Street and that was where she wanted to go. Trevor was flabbergasted with the sights, but Li was fascinated with the clothes young people were wearing. Back in the hotel she was making sketches of the clothes, Trevor had never seen her draw before and he was impressed. They saw most of the sights, but Li wanted to go back to Carnaby Street.

During the next few weeks Trevor and his father argued often and John was cold to Li. Trevor could not find a suitable job and was frustrated. He told Li they had to go back to Hong Kong he was unhappy with everything in Birmingham including the climate. Li was adjusting to the climate but if her husband said they must go then they must go. When they were leaving Li told her father-in-law he should come to Hong Kong, even Trevor was surprised.

The stopover in Singapore was a great pleasure, suddenly Trevor felt free. Li and Nur had a lot to discuss. Li was talking about clothes, double decker buses and the climate. She was telling Nur she had to see England. Trevor was telling Charley about his problems trying to find a job. Every time he had an interview they asked about his military record and then saw his discharge, so no job. Charley's advice was to go back to Hong Kong and work with his wife and try jobs with Chinese companies, forget British companies.

Back in Hong Kong Meng was kissing them both with such ferocity Li told her to calm down. Trevor realized England was a bad idea and Meng had showed him Hong Kong was his place. After a couple of weeks he had a job looking at the books of a Chinese company and then more customers for his accountancy company. Li was producing some way-out clothes she had seen in London and was collecting new customers. Meng was a bit sceptical with these new styles but was convinced by this new surge in customers.

One night Trevor went to a local bar, his day had been hectic, and he needed a cold beer. There he met one of his old barmen. After a couple of beers this man told him the story of the robbery. One of the barmen needed money as he had a gambling problem. There was a fire in one of the bars and Trevor had gone to help put out the fire. He had taken off his top tunic and the man had found the keys. He had made an imprint of the keys. After a couple weeks the man had hidden in the store on a Friday night, robbed the tills and slipped out as the cleaners came in on the Saturday morning. This man only knew this about two months later when the man was drunk late one night. He had tried to contact Trevor, but he had gone to England.

"I should have him killed for he has ruined my life."

"No need sergeant his gambling problem did not stop, his debts mounted, and he has been disposed of."

Trevor could not visualize the man, but he had been disposed of, suddenly Trevor had a feeling of sympathy. It cleared a problem in his past. He found Osborn had a new commander and he was not going to be help in clearing Trevor's name. Trevor now decided that this old problem was dead and buried. Now for his next problem, Li had invited his father to come to Hong Kong. His father had written to say he would come for a visit and if he liked it, he might stay. He was tired of being alone, the area was changing and even the pub was not the same. Li had explained to Trevor that she only had three relatives and it was her duty to help them all.

Li and Meng got together and leased a flat next door to Meng and if John liked it, they could get a permanent lease. Meng seemed to be excited about having a relative nearby. Trevor was not sure about this situation as his father was much too young to retire. At least John would not be living with him and Li.

Trevor's other problem was that although he and Li had regular intercourse, she could not get pregnant. The doctor could find nothing wrong with either of them, so they were looking into adoption. There was an orphanage nearby and they visited it regularly. Li wanted a baby or a child not more than one year old. Trevor did not have any conditions he was just so sad to see all the unwanted children. The orphanage had a newborn boy, but the legal process could take months. They could foster the boy on the understanding they may not be able to keep him if the adoption process failed. What worried Trevor was his dishonourable discharge. He was now running a profitable accounting company and Li and Meng had the clothing company. If necessary, he would try to find the barman who had explained the robbery (opening old wounds) he was prepared to go through it all again.

John and this baby arrived at about the same time and Li decided to call the baby Johnathon, she had been looking at English names. Trevor smiled to himself when she announced the name. Li said they would give him other Chinese names when they were sure that the baby was theirs. She had decorated a second bedroom and bought a cot, there was also a single bed for night feeds. Trevor realized he was now sharing Li with Johnathon, but he was not jealous.

Trevor and Meng met John at the airport and gave Li's apologizes as she was looking after the baby. Trevor explained that they were fostering the child. John was very friendly to Meng, and she shook his hand. Trevor left Meng to talk to his father while he arranged the baggage and transport. Trevor was looking at the baggage and thinking his father was planning to stay. They dropped the luggage at John's new flat and went to Trevor's place. Li had food, cold beer and champagne ready for the celebration. John gave Li a peck on the cheek and consumed a beer explaining he was very thirsty. John told them he had not tasted champagne for many years. Before the war he had been to France with the army and visited Rheims and a place where they bottled champagne. They had sampled quite a bit of their produce and he was wondering whether he had a taste for it after these many years. Trevor was watching his father charm the two sisters.

Meng took John to his new home and said she would look after him. During the next few days Meng was treating John like he was her father. She took him to the races and a football match. One of her customers had a workshop and John was used to operating lathes and was offered a job. He was asked to manage the workshop and he wrote a letter of resignation to his employers in England. Trevor was watching all these events and shaking his head. Meng asked Li if she could look after their sewing business while she showed John around. They were going on a cruise around the harbour and then the next day on a fishing trip. Trevor could not believe what was happening and of course Li was looking after the baby, so he had to make his own way.

John started work and things settled down and Trevor took his father to a bar in a big hotel.

"Do you think you can stay and work here in Hong Kong?"

"I love it here, the climate is a bit difficult, but I don't have to work too hard. I am talking to the owner about buying a new lathe so we can expand the business. I wondered what it would be like working for a Chinese owner, but he is great he accepts all my suggestions. The workers are very friendly, and I go home to a neighbour who does anything I ask. I wish I had had a daughter now I treat her like a daughter. I wonder why she is not married because she deserves a good husband."

This was a new father, and he was drinking less; Meng drank very little. Now he could concentrate on the adoption process. Johnathon was a very happy baby, he hardly ever cried. It turned out that the adoption process was much quicker than he had expected. There were so many orphans the system was trying to reduce the numbers as quickly as possible. Trevor was looking at all those older children and wondering whether they should adopt another child.

While he was turning these possibilities over in his mind there was a new development.

Li received a letter from her uncle Chen who lived in Vancouver. She had written him a few letters mainly about developments in the family. She had mentioned that she had been to England and had worked in a restaurant in Birmingham. Uncle Chen had a restaurant and as he was getting old, he needed help. Li reminded Trevor that if a family member needed help it was her duty to go to their aid. Trevor had an assistant who could keep his business running; this young man had seemed a likely candidate for Meng's husband. Trevor was no matchmaker and told himself to stay out of other people's affairs.

Trevor told his father they were going to Vancouver and would he be okay.

"Son I am living a new life and regretting my age. I can't believe what I have missed. I awake in the morning and happily go to work. I come home and I am free and can go anywhere. If I need company, I just call Meng and she knows all the best restaurants and fun places to go. Yes, son go do your thing I will be okay."

Trevor, Li and Johnathon took a ship to Vancouver and Johnathon was good most of the voyage; he slept almost all the way. Li was enjoying the variety of food. There were very few Chinese dishes, but she was eating food she had never eaten. As they entered Vancouver harbour Trevor could hardly believe the sight. It was so different from Hong Kong; it was so uncluttered with boats and looked so clean. Looking past the city he could see mountains with snow on the peaks. He was excited to see this city and one of the sailors said he could ski in the winter. He had not seen snow since he was a child, he had lived most of his adult life in hot tropical places. Heavier clothes would be necessary for himself, Li and Johnathon. Li was also enthralled with the sights; Johnathon was too young to give an opinion.

They were met at the dock by Uncle Chen. He had a sign saying Uncle Chen. Trevor thought that very funny. He was a small slim balding man dressed in a well-tailored dark suit. Trevor saw the joy in his face when he greeted Li and Johnathon, Trevor introduced himself in Cantonese.

Uncle Chen stood back then warmly shook Trevor's hand and said, "I think you speak Cantonese better than me. Most of the time I am talking English and only when I go deep into Chinatown do I speak Cantonese."

He then ushered them to a large chauffeur driven car.

"Don't worry this is not my car I have borrowed it from a friend."

They arrived at a large two storey house and the door was opened by Chen's house maid Wei. They were all introduced and then ushered into the dining room where there was a spread of food and champagne, there was also red caviar. Trevor liked the red caviar but did not like the black caviar, Li had never tasted Caviar. Wei asked if she could hold Johnathon, Li was surprised she asked in English. Chen explained she was from northern China and Mandarin was her natural language, she had lived in Canada since a child and so they spoke in English. Wei did everything including keeping the household accounts.

Wei took Johnathon and he did not cry he loved her necklace.

"By the way I like the name Johnathon it sounds sophisticated. He seems a good boy. I regret not having children but by the time I married I was too old. Wei has bought lots of things for the boy and I see the delight in her face when she holds him. I have to go to the restaurant, so you just relax. Tomorrow being Sunday the restaurant is closed, and we can sit down and have a long chat."

Trevor thought if he closed his eyes, he was listening to an Englishman using phrases like 'a long chat'. Li was showing him what Wei had collected for Johnathon. She had nappies, powdered milk of several kinds, jars of baby foods and bottles with teats. Li told Trevor that this lady was amazing, she had already changed a nappy and fed Johnathon. They all slept soundly that night and Chen had told them not to wait up for him as he would be very late.

In the morning Wei had breakfast ready and she had already fed Johnathon. Chen explained that she did not normally work on Sunday, but she insisted on working this Sunday. Chen decided that before the chat he would take them in his car and show them Vancouver. His 51 Buick was very comfortable and easily seated them all including Wei. Trevor and Li noticed how quiet and clean the city was and there appeared to be very few shops open. Chen pointed out his restaurant which was near the edge of Chinatown. He then drove to a park near the harbour. They all got out of the car to admire the view; Chen pointed out the University and some of the neighbourhoods. Trevor was entranced by this harbour, it seemed that there was nothing on it except a couple of yachts. Back at the house Chen said they should have tea and listen to his story.

"I escaped China in 1947 and came to Canada. I came to Vancouver as I knew there were many Chinese here. I worked several jobs but made sure I learnt English. Without English the first year was rough; I was at the mercy of Chinese who had been here a long time. I was a waiter, a cleaner and a cook in those first years. As a waiter I met a Canadian and we spoke in English. I was glad to improve my English. He was opening a restaurant and offered me a job. That job was a revelation. I was paid a fair wage and treated with respect. That man is my best friend and I want to visit him when I get the time. It took me four years to buy my first car, the one we used today."

"How did you learn to drive."

"Again, my Canadian friend taught me to drive and put me on to a good mechanic, also one of my friends. It seemed it was easier to make friends with Canadians than Chinese who were struggling to make a living. The rich Chinese were not friendly, and I learned to ignore them. After a few more years, I decided to open a restaurant with my friend, which was just outside Chinatown but as you see Chinatown has grown around me. I wanted to cook Cantonese food as well as some dishes the Canadians would like. My clientele was a mixed bunch but lately Chinese are coming to eat Cantonese food. Let's have tea I am getting thirsty."

"Uncle this is a fascinating story, and we want to listen to more, but we have a problem. All our clothes are suitable for Hong Kong but not Vancouver."

"Ah my son, can you imagine I had the same problem when I arrived from Canton, and I had no money. You have stirred a memory. I have arranged for a tailor to visit tomorrow; he is another friend, an Indian. Wei will take you shopping for clothes later tomorrow; she has her own car."

They drank their tea and Johnathon amused them for a while.

"I worked hard for many years and when I was settled, I decided to find a wife. I found a widow whose mother was Chinese, and her father was Russian. They had come from Harbin in North China. We tried to have a child, but my wife died. I met Wei through my wife; she is half Chinese and half Russian. She will tell you her story. Anyway I thought I was too old to have children, so I suppose time slipped away. I have talked a lot so maybe it is Wei's turn."

"I was born in Harbin and came to Vancouver as a young girl. Harbin was a Russian town in China and at home we spoke Russian. When we first came to Canada, I spoke Russian and Mandarin. I went to school here and quickly learned English; in fact, I was teaching my parents English. I was going to get married to a Russian boy and he went to earn money in the mines in the Yukon. Unfortunately he was killed, and I decided to remain single. Your uncle gave me a job in his restaurant, he liked my English. He saw I was not a real waitress material and as he had bought a new house, he offered me a job as housekeeper. I love my job as I have freedom in what I do and when I do it. Most of the guests who come to this house are Canadians and they treat me as an equal. Your uncle works many hours and I have told him to slow down. He told me about his niece in Hong Kong and I told him to invite you."

"Do you live near here?"

"Yes, I live with my aging parents, and they just love this country. They will have gone to the Russian Orthodox Church today, but I am glad to be here."

Now Li wanted to tell her story.

"My mother decided to escape Canton so my mother, me and my sister walked to Hong Kong. I am not sure how we got across the border, but we arrived in Hong Kong with little money. My sister and I did have some English as we had been to a missionary school. We found a church and they gave us food and shelter. The long trek had taken its toll on our mother and she died. The doctor said she had TB and was surprised she could walk from Canton. Meng went to work while I went to the church school. After one year I had to go to work, but I thank the church for giving me a start."

At one place in the story Trevor looked at Chen and there were tears running down his face.

"With both of us working we could get a place of our own although it was very meagre. We were both working at sewing machines ten hours a day and had no energy for a social life. As we grew older and more experienced, we decided that if we bought a sewing machine we could make more money. One night we went to a dance at the church. We only allowed ourselves one night to relax. At a table was a tall Englishman but most of the patrons were Chinese with one or two older European couples. He asked me for a dance; he was not very good, but I liked the feeling. The next week he danced with me and my sister, and I learned he was in the army. My first reaction was that army meant trouble, but he was so kind. When he proposed I was in shock but accepted and never regretted it."

At this point Chen rose from his seat and hugged Trevor. After lunch the discussion resumed. Johnathon was sitting in his highchair and seemingly enjoying the talk.

"The reason I invited you to Vancouver is that I need a rest. I want you to take over the restaurant so I can see Canada. You should see Canada before me. I want you to take the train to Toronto as they have the biggest Chinatown. I want you to eat there and look at their menus and possibly bring some back. My restaurant needs a change and I want it to appeal to Canadians. If you want to take Johnathon okay but Wei is prepared to take care of him." "Thank you Uncle. I have every faith in Wei, but I could not be away from him for more than a few days."

"Well said, I would love to have him, but you are his mother."

The next day the tailor came and told them he could do women's clothing as well as men's. Shopping for other clothes including underwear was a delight but Li noticed there was no 'way out' clothing she was making in Hong Kong, it was nearly all conservative clothing. Li showed Wei some of her sketches and Wei told her there was a small hippie community in Vancouver.

Trevor was enjoying the cleanliness and the politeness of the people they met. Wei was such a good driver better than Uncle Chen. The traffic was slow and easy, nothing like Hong Kong. Trevor was thinking this city was the ideal place to live, no way did he want to go back to Hong Kong.

The train to Toronto was a pleasure. They had a sleeping cabin with a window. Li had rarely been on a train and Trevor had never been on such a long journey. This journey made Li and Trevor realize the size of Canada. Johnathon was no problem as the rocking of the train had him sleeping most of the time.

Toronto was a much more vibrant city and with their hotel close to Chinatown it made walking about the area easy. The hotel had a nurse who could look after Johnathon in the evening. They were sampling Chinese food at lunch time and in the evening; there were also collecting menus. They had little recourse to try their Cantonese but one night Trevor tried his Cantonese. The restaurant went quiet and then a man started clapping. Trevor was surprised that this man was not Chinese. There was only one minor problem in one of the restaurants. Trevor was on his way to the toilets when approaching two waiters he heard one say to the other in Cantonese "who is that woman with this man?"

"That is my wife so be careful what you say."

His reply in Cantonese had them open mouthed and they quickly retreated to the kitchen.

Johnathon loved the trip on a harbour cruise he was very animated. Trevor was still wondering at the emptiness of the harbour; he was still referring everything back to Hong Kong. Li noticed how everyone enjoyed the buffet with wine.

After a few days they booked a flight to Vancouver. Li had a window seat and was enjoying the flight as most of it was cloudless. Johnathon had his own seat and was amusing the stewardesses. Trevor was reviewing his life and deciding he wanted to stay in this country. His thoughts went to his father and then to his mother. Li would not leave her adopted son and yet his mother had left him.

Back in Vancouver Chen was delighted with their report and loved reading the new menus. Li wanted to see the restaurant and Trevor wanted to see the books. Chen was over the moon and was willing to do everything that was going to change his restaurant. Chen explained that many people had told him that closing on a Sunday was a mistake. He decided that people traffic in the city was slow on a Sunday, but things were changing.

Li suggested that they would advertise a buffet with two glasses of wine for a flat fee and this was ideal for a Sunday opening. Chen was a bit sceptical, but he wanted his niece to try anything. Li set up an advertising board a couple of days in advance. That Sunday was a fantastic success, and many bottles of wine were consumed, most people liked more than two glasses. Most of the customers were Canadians but a few Chinese came. One Chinese man asked who had organized this event. Li talked to the man while Chen watched in the background. Li was talking to an underworld figure and when Trevor talked to him in Cantonese he went away smiling. This event happened every other Sunday and Li talked Chen in to closing on Tuesdays to give the staff a rest.

Trevor was now setting up his accountancy business. His certificates from Hong Kong were accepted as was his army driving license. They bought a car and now his first trip was to the mountains. He determined he would ski in the winter. Each year they went skiing and Li was better at it than Trevor. Chen advised they should become citizens as soon as possible. Trevor and Li had no problem with becoming Canadian citizens.

News from Hong Kong was good, now Meng had an English father she was getting many suitors. John was vetting the suitors. John was in charge of the workshop and business was expanding much to the delight of the owner. John had decided to sell his house in England, and he took Meng to England in case she wanted anything. He wanted nothing and the contents would go to the rubbish dump or to charity. Meng loved England and had made John take her to Carnaby Street.

Li was running the restaurant and she decided to change most of the menu and was getting mainly

Canadian customers. Chen did not care he wanted to travel and see Canada. He was going to visit the man who gave him his break. This man had a cabin on Manitoulin Island in Ontario. Li was worried he might get lost. He had changed his will and Li would get most except a large sum for Wei. He laughingly told Li he was going to spend her inheritance.

Trevor employed two young people to help him with his business, they were both university graduates. One was a Canadian boy of English extraction and the other a Chinese girl. On reflection he wondered whether he was match making but let them get on with their work. Trevor and Li were now Canadian citizens and Trevor was talking about standing for Parliament.

News from Manitoulin was good. Chen had been fishing, something he had not done since a boy. Now he had a sophisticated rod and reel. He loved the barbecues; previously he had eaten little meat. What made him so proud was that people who had talked to him on the phone were surprised when he met them; he was Chinese.

Wei was having fun chasing Johnathon about; she loved that boy. She talked Li into thinking about adopting a little girl. As a single woman she could not adopt and loved children. Li talked to Trevor who was all for the idea.

"We will have a real Canadian in the family and

when she comes, we will invite my father and Meng to see this wonderful country. We are staying here forever."

Milton Keynes UK
Ingram Content Group UK Ltd.
UKHW040842030823
426261UK00001B/6